T0147700

Also by Leon Arden

Novels:

The Savage Place
Seesaw Sunday
The Twilight's Last Gleaming
One Fine Day
The Walk to the Paradise Garden

Plays:

The Midnight Ride of Alvin Blum (with Donald Honig)

THE ICE CHILD

AND OTHER STORIES

LEON ARDEN

THE ICE CHILD
AND OTHER STORIES

This is a work of fiction. All of the characters, names, incidents, organizations, and dialogue in this novel are either the products of the author's imagination or are used fictitiously.

iUniverse books may be ordered through booksellers or by contacting:

iUniverse
1663 Liberty Drive
Bloomington, IN 47403
www.iuniverse.com
1-800-Authors (1-800-288-4677)

Because of the dynamic nature of the Internet, any web addresses or links contained in this book may have changed since publication and may no longer be valid. The views expressed in this work are solely those of the author and do not necessarily reflect the views of the publisher, and the publisher hereby disclaims any responsibility for them.

Any people depicted in stock imagery provided by Thinkstock are models, and such images are being used for illustrative purposes only. Certain stock imagery © Thinkstock.

ISBN: 978-1-4917-7282-9 (sc)
ISBN: 978-1-4917-7281-2 (e)

Library of Congress Control Number: 2015911612

Print information available on the last page.

iUniverse rev. date: 07/17/2015

Sources

"Coming of Age," *Woman's Realm* (England) also Woman's Day (Australia) and Femina (South Africa); "Getting through to Him," *Cosmopolitan* (Australia) renamed "Come Live With Me and Be My Love"; "The Book Collector," *Modern Maturity* (California); "A Feminine Ending," *Woman's Weekly* (South Africa); "The Ice Child," *Auguries* (England); "If Music Be the Food of Love," *Passager* (United States)

This one is for Charles Palliser

CONTENTS

Coming of Age

They saw a distant steeple behind the hills, then the same steeple, larger, amid a clutch of roofs, and finally they drove into a cobbled street where the church stood, its cracked steps leading down to a dog lying in the road, dead. Their daughter would have been most upset had she been there to see it. Yet what a relief to stop after a long drive. In the stillness they could smell newly baked bread. Children were gaping at them with impudent innocence.

"You'd think they'd never seen tourists before," Cordelia said.

"Maybe they haven't."

"Oh, they must have done."

"In a remote place like this?" her husband asked. "Not often."

Perhaps he was right since they were his compatriots, not hers, who swarmed down here in the thousands. Not that many English got to Mexico. She glanced again at the directions the lady in the hotel had given them.

"It says to turn right at the church and head out of town again."

Harvey waved as they drove away. The children, too bemused to respond, just watched. A distant mountain range was out of focus in the purple mist, and the foothills seemed heavily sprinkled with pepper and salt. It had all grown lovely again with that capacity for abrupt change that was so typical here.

They found the ranch without trouble. There was a barn, a fence, and, sure enough, horses. Harvey got out as if the long ride had aged him. His wife took longer, having turned the rearview mirror on

1

herself. When she joined him at the fence, a shabby, unshaven man, in appearance more beggar than landowner, approached them in his own sweet time. Though it must have become quickly evident to him that the woman spoke Spanish and the man did not, he continued to reply only to Harvey though Cordelia asked the questions and translated his replies. Twenty dollars for two horses for two days. That included a guide. Harvey was more than happy with this.

"He says we can start in five minutes."

"In Mexico that means half an hour. Let's go back and get some food. Might be a long haul till lunch."

"He's one of those men who think women don't exist," she complained as they headed again in the direction of the steeple. Harvey pointed out that he was a typical Mexican: the man was the head of the family; the man made the decisions.

"Exactly," she said, "women don't exist."

Again he worried that their holiday would go sour. He thought of Lake Patzcuaro, where, two days ago, they had spent a wonderful morning walking by the shore as the valley had become slowly unchilled in the subtle sunlight, the netwinged boats like frail birds come to rest on the water.

Back in their car, he had stopped so his wife could ask directions of a green-eyed Indian woman with a baby in her arms. The woman had pointed on ahead, silently. They'd thanked her and had been about to drive off when she'd stepped closer to the window, peering in at Cordelia with a query of her own. He'd heard the Indian say, "Muy bonita," more than once and his wife's insistent "No gracias." But then his wife had given the woman some money. "Let's go now, please," Cordelia had said, turning to him with a strained look. As they'd left, the receding eyes, like luminous green marbles, had watched them.

"What was she selling?"

"The baby."

After a while he'd asked, "Was it hers?"

"She said she needed the money to feed the others."

"Good God."

Although they had both been shaken, it hadn't soured Mexico for her as he'd feared it would.

Opposite the church and its lifeless dog, they found boxes of fruit and bread guarded by a mute woman seated on a stool from whom they bought one mango and two rolls. Eager to buy a hat in case of rain, he could find nowhere to go for such an item though impressive wide-brimmed Stetsons atop gloomy Indians floated this way and that.

"They forever try to sell you things you don't want," he groused, while driving back, "but, of course, once you're in real need, all commerce ends."

"Oh, a little rain won't hurt you," she said in that maddening way of hers of suddenly becoming blissfully free of all his concerns. To pass a man leading a burro, he glanced in the rearview mirror and found, thanks to her attempt to turn it back to its previous angle, not the road but his own ungainly face.

At the ranch, two horses were saddled. Again the owner finally appeared. Harvey put the food in his saddlebag and asked his wife where their guide was. She spoke to the owner. "He says this one will take us."

Harvey saw a child was waiting for them. The boy stood there thin as sticks, barefoot in his poncho, and looking about as useful as a busted balloon. The horse he stood near had not yet been saddled. Harvey was about to say, "No children," when the boy, without warning, became an effortless flow of mercury until he was astride the horse, bareback, like Zapata himself. His longish, tar-black hair was held back with string. His small mask of milk chocolate had the familiar look of monumental resignation.

The owner spoke. "He wishes *you* a pleasant trip," Cordelia said, with pointed irony.

"Come on, let's go."

"He also says it would be good to tip the child later."

When the ranch was out of sight, Harvey galloped. Here at last was true adventure. He stopped when he looked back and saw his wife bouncing uncontrollably like a rodeo rider atop a wild horse.

"Don't do that," she snapped at him when she had caught up.

"I forgot that when one runs they all run."

"Remember it. Please!"

Although the boy had flown into the lead, he kept watch on them and now cantered back, unable to resist a smile.

Soon slippery mud made even walking the animals difficult. They went in single file following the boy through the gullies of low hills and scrubland. Then into woods and out again. There was no view. Occasionally a Mexican would appear on foot and say "'Dios" as he passed.

"If they're such friendly people," she said with a smile, "why do they say good-bye as soon as they meet you?"

"Ask him."

She did. "He says they're saying 'God,' as in 'Go with God.'"

"Of course, yes."

"I asked him his name. He's called Twig. I think that's what he said."

"How does he spell it?"

She lowered her voice. "I asked. He can't read."

"What's his age?"

"Same as Jess."

"Eleven? Looks smaller."

"Much smaller."

They went on silently for a while, the boy leading until it began to rain. He stopped and spoke. Cordelia looked into her saddlebag and pulled out a poncho. There was one in Harvey's too. He felt a bit foolish fitting it over his head. This was forgotten when he discovered how protected he was from the cutting wind as they came to the crest of a hill and a view of the valley before heading down beneath an offcolored sky.

The mention of Jess had sent Cordelia's thoughts far afield. "Do you think she's all right?" That was the question, always. He said he was sure of it. Really sure? Yes, of course he was. Their daughter, Jessica, had been left behind with his parents in New York. To Cordelia, that city's year-round open season for rape and murder was worrying enough. But his parents were hopeless. Even in the safety of their flat there was cause for worry. Jess would be spoiled rotten by American permissiveness and made fat by American ice cream. She was annoyed that Harvey didn't understand this. "Look what a cock-up they made of you," she said.

They each thought the other worried too much because they worried over different things. When flying, she was engrossed with death; he, the cost of the flight. When eating, he was obsessed with cholesterol; she, the number of calories. But, separately and together, they both worried full-time about Jess. When Harvey dismissed concerns involving his parents or the dangers of New York, he did so for Cordelia's sake, keeping his fears to himself just as he kept to himself those old stories of bandits in the Mexican hills.

As the rain stopped, they came upon fences and more people saying "Dios" and finally a bleak, shabby village. It was so primitive there was no road leading to it, and yet there, before them, was a large Coca-Cola sign held aloft by posts in a field. They dismounted in the plaza onto weak legs and sat down. The boy brought them canned sardines, fresh bread, and warm Coke. The aroma stunned them. They had never had a more delicious feast. The boy brought the horses together and emptied numerous bottles of Coke into each large, uplifted mouth. He went about seeing to it that they all were taken care of without himself stopping to eat or drink.

Cordelia marveled at the self-sufficiency of someone no older than their daughter, who couldn't take care of herself and wouldn't take care of her room. She asked if he was going to eat now, and he said, "Sí, momentito," and went off in his small bare feet. He soon returned, sat with his back against a wall, and, looking at nothing in particular, took discreet bites out of his bread and cheese. Children watched them from a distance, frozen with amazement. Cordelia grinned, and one of them, a little girl, cringed in a blissful, gap-toothed smile. At his wife's insistence, Harvey gave the child their rolls to share among them. The mango had proved to be rotten.

To help Cordelia into her saddle, Harvey pushed with both palms on her buttocks. His horse too seemed to have grown in height. He climbed the animal like a wall. Could it really be that he was getting old?

"Do you think she goes to school?" his wife asked of the little one to whom he had given away their food. He didn't know. But the question sent her thoughts back again to Jess. Had they made the right choice in sending her to an all-girls school over one that was mixed? They talked about this for a while and got no further with it on horseback than they had all the other times they had dredged through the subject in their flat in Belsize Park.

They lived in London because Cordelia had a job there as a journalist. He had been sent overseas as a salesman for an American film company. They'd met at a health-food restaurant, and the next evening he'd taken her to a private showing of *Under the Volcano.*

To Harvey she'd evoked any number of elegant English film actresses who had mesmerized him in his early New York youth. To her he had been an entertaining, roughhewn original who, though wanting polishing like many lumbering Americans, only occasionally became an actual social hazard. His emotions, however, had been refreshingly free from restraint. For a time everything had seemed deceptively uncomplicated. England had agreed with him, as marriage had with her.

Having a child would also agree with him, she'd said, and soon he had been happily astride a runaway horse called parenthood. What he hadn't been told was that the gallop never ceased and that each day was a race toward the end of something endless. Their daughter had transformed their lives as they'd known she would but in ways they would not have been able to guess. She freed them from self-obsession and certainty. She opened up a vast and complex world while enabling them to extract great pleasure from the very simplest of things. She deepened at a stroke their understanding of life and renewed, as never before, their acquaintance with dread. Their daughter was always with them even when she was somewhere else. The very fact of her existence was as if she were constantly crying in a carry-cot at their feet. And when she was somewhere else, the dread was worse.

"Oh, look, look," she called to him from her saddle. "How beautiful."

Coming upon a lake, they had frightened off some geese who slapped the water with each loud beat of their wings as they raced across the surface leaving double rows of widening circles until furiously lifting off and sliding into the sky. Their young guide flapped his arms and laughed, not at the birds but at the pleasure they gave Cordelia. She reached across from her saddle and patted his head.

While crossing a landscape reminiscent of the African veldt, she talked to the boy for a while, then said to her husband, "He has three brothers. One's dead. One's in Texas. One's in jail. He explained why, but I couldn't follow. When he grows up, he wants to work in a big hotel where rich Americans stay. His mother was hurt in the earthquake—when was it, two years ago? He likes the music of Michael Jackson. And he wants to know why we're not taking snaps like the other tourists."

"Did you tell him our camera was stolen the day we arrived?"

"Yes."

"What did he say?"

"He said people should not steal."

"A moral philosopher."

"I tried to tell him we weren't out of pocket because of the insurance."

"And?"

"He doesn't know what insurance is."

The boy turned in his saddle to see if they were following.

"Oh, his face is so beautiful," she said. "Wouldn't he make a lovely brother for Jess?"

"And I bet he'd keep his room tidy too."

At dusk Harvey began to understand how men could sleep in their saddles. Cordelia didn't seem half as tired. *Is this what turning forty does?* he wondered. He cheered up when she said, "God, I'm exhausted." But he regretted the rolls given away to those children. Increasingly, he had trouble seeing the path. They had damn well better get to where they were going, he thought, or they'd be lost in the dark.

"Here we are," Cordelia's voice called out, and before them loomed a clutch of huts where an old woman was cooking food over an open fire inside what, to Harvey, resembled a shabby imitation of a baseball dugout.

Sitting like benched rookies waiting for a chance at bat, they each ate a steaming plateful of painfully spicy enchiladas and refried beans. The request for a drink to cool the furnace of his mouth was a serious mistake; a gulp of warm Coke all but lifted off the top of his head. He gave up drinking and just ate. Then he gave up eating and just sat. After unsaddling the horses and leading them away, the boy returned to ask Harvey a question. Cordelia, using his thigh as a pillow, had to be shaken awake to translate. The boy wanted to know if they were ready to sleep.

Even his wife, who enjoyed camping far more than he, found the empty storage room abysmal. It smelled of dried mud and farmyard animals. "Wants doing up," she said. Harvey was too exhausted to speak. They lay on mats, each wrapped in a blanket, wearing their shoes for warmth. Somewhere a baby cried without stopping. When Harvey woke hours later, the night had grown solid with cold. There was movement next to him. "Are you warm enough?" he asked. "No," she said, as if the fault were his. They pushed the straw mats together and rolled themselves into both blankets like a single bundle. Was it better this way? "We'll see" was her reply. He kissed her. "Yes, it's better this way." Her body was small like a well-made watch. Greater size or weight would have been to no advantage. Styling and quality was all. "Nice," she said and was asleep again.

The door swung open, slicing the room with morning light. They blinked at bare feet and two twigs for legs. He bid them each good morning, and after he went out, scraping the door shut, they hobbled about amused by their infirmities like old people who knew they would soon be young again.

Mounted on horses, they entered a blue, moist, cool day. A man on a chair in an open field was having his hair cut. At noon they arrived at a stream near a clearing in the woods. In the warm sun, they sat eating fruit and cheese as the boy took the horses down to the water.

Harvey stared after him. "Hard to imagine *him* being afraid of the dark."

After musing for a bit, she said, "You know, I really do think we should take her to see someone."

"You really want to get into all that?"

She nodded, and he said no more. When the boy returned, leading the horses, Cordelia was attending to a slipped contact lens, and Harvey was throwing left jabs at the leaf of a low-hanging branch. The boy smiled and hit out with his fist at the leaf of a much-lower branch. Becoming his coach, Harvey changed the boy's stance and taught him to bend and jab with his left while keeping his right at the ready. He was such a good student that they boxed each other for a few moments with ferocious exaggeration, neither trying to land a blow.

When Cordelia was ready, it was time to leave. Because the animals were nervous, the boy held the reins as she mounted. Harvey climbed on and then waited with fascination to observe once again that nonchalant jump-float onto a saddleless horse. The boy stood in position, patting the smooth, brown hair of the enormous neck. Then he stopped and became terribly still. His attention had been riveted to the middle distance as if by a miraculous annunciation.

Harvey turned and saw a man standing among the trees. A rent in the left leg of his trousers hung open like a door flap. His tongue was at work inside his mouth as if he had just finished eating. He held a machete, resting it in the dirt like a cane. Harvey noticed two other men: a fat one in a pair of overalls too small for him, a straw hat perched high on his head, and another squatting to pick something out of the dirt, then tossing it away. In his other hand he held a knife.

Cordelia said, "Oh dear, my sunglasses," and climbed down to get them as Harvey called out, "No, don't." Too late. Now she, standing beside her horse, also saw them. She turned to her husband, her face sagging with fear.

"Get mounted," he told her. The fat one barked something, and she froze.

"Ask him what he wants."

She did, and when the man with the machete responded, Cordelia lurched slightly. "Oh my God, oh my God," she whispered.

"What?" Harvey called out. "What? What did he say?"

The fat one said something to the boy. All three were watching him now, perhaps assessing his resourcefulness in these empty woods, knowing that these others, for whom he was the guide, were helpless.

"What did he say to him?" Harvey asked in hushed desperation.

Before his wife could answer, the boy began emitting a sound that rose in a steady whine, private and pitiful, as he sank to his knees, his face at last revealing what he really was: a child. "*Padre*," he wailed. This pleased the three men, and they smiled at each other.

"What's happening?" Harvey cried. "Will you tell me what's happening?"

At that moment the earth jumped, the horses went crazy, Harvey was spun about, Cordelia knocked over. A veil of dust inundated everything. "Aheeeeeeee!" This from the man with the machete. He was sitting on the ground, eyes closed, pressing with both hands on his right thigh. The fat one backed away, then ran, losing his hat. The third man was already gone. On his knees, both hands holding the gun, the boy studied the wounded man and then spoke, ending with *"Por favor."* The glistening machete was tossed forward. The boy found a safe slot for it in Harvey's saddle, then slipped his gun under his poncho. As if there was safety in heights, a trembling Cordelia, with the boy's help, scrambled onto her horse. Then he swiftly levitated onto his own. Beckoning, he led the way in a diligent canter.

Harvey caught up to his wife to ask if she was all right. She could barely speak, and they held hands for a time. Then she told him what the bandit had said. The money first, then the woman. And the boy would be killed if he didn't obey. They held hands until the path narrowed and their horses pulled them apart. He wanted to stay near to reassure her. But the boy was the one she wished to be near. Last in line, Harvey kept looking behind him, his back growing cold in the midday heat.

Cordelia talked rapidly in Spanish, asking many questions.

"He thinks we're quite safe. Says they're probably cowards. If they are not cowards, he will shoot at them again, so not to worry. How can he be so bloody calm? He doesn't know who they are and doesn't care. I asked how he could take us out knowing this might happen. It's never happened before, he said. Then why did his father give him a gun in the first place? It's so nothing happens to us, right? No, he said. It's so nothing happens to the horses."

As his heartbeat lessened, Harvey's sense of uselessness diminished. That their lives rested in this boy's palm seemed extraordinary. What a relief that Jess wasn't with them.

Above was a panoply of foliage through which light dabbed with flecks of gaiety and sudden, frequent sun-streaks of joy. Shambolic relief settled upon him with its volatile sense of peace. They were alive. It was sinking in. Up ahead, waiting eagerly, was the rest of his life. Flying home, hugging Jessica, and putting to use a vast, unimaginable extravagance of time.

Later on, his voice low, Harvey asked, "Did he shoot to kill, or what?"

"He aimed at that rip in his trousers."

"Well, as you would say, we'll dine out on this one."

"We're not home yet. And I want to talk to that boy's father."

"Oh, I'd like to clock him one."

When they had been out of the woods for some time, the boy asked them to wait and rode to some high ground. There he stood on his horse like a circus performer and looked back. Cordelia finished off an apple while they waited. He returned, smiling. But when he saw that she had thrown the core into the path, he slid disapprovingly from his horse, tossed the telltale item out of sight of possible pursuers, jumped, clutching his horse with his legs, straightened up, and rode on.

"You know," Harvey said, "when he grows up, he's going to be dynamite."

"Maybe, if he can make it to America."

The feeling that they were now almost surely safe didn't keep him from gasping, or her from screaming, when a man appeared in front of them, said, "*Dios*," and walked on.

At the ranch, Cordelia was angry to find the owner gone. Probably went to town, the boy said. There was nothing for it but to pay and leave. While the boy unsaddled the horses, a quiet discussion ensued over what the tip should be. They decided on a large sum, larger than Harvey wished. Cordelia smiled brightly and handed over the money. The boy kept nodding, eyes wide, saying "Muchas gracias" many times. She chatted a bit more. He responded at length. When one of the horses wandered, he hurried to fetch it.

But something had happened. Cordelia looked lost, as if unsure of who or where she was. Her eyes met her husband's without noticing him. For a moment she was not seeing; she was understanding.

"Did you hear what he said?" she asked.

"No."

"I told him he's a very brave boy."

"And …?"

"And he said he isn't a boy. He's a girl."

"A girl?"

They watched her leading the animals to a trough of water. She lifted each saddle to balance it on the fence. Looking up, she saw them watching. A moment's hesitation, a wave of her hand. Caught gaping like rude tourists, they also waved, walked to their car, and drove up a hill to the paved road. There they stopped and looked back.

She was riding again, she and her horse lifting gracefully and floating weightlessly over the fence to bounce down into the dust and ride forth, turning, cantering, gaining speed, and flying back over the same fence as if nature, compensating for her size, had given her magic powers to lift that great beast and set it down again whenever she wished.

"Shall we go?" Cordelia asked. "A hot bath would be lovely."

"And dinner with a bottle of wine."

"And a proper bed."

But they kept watching the girl on the jumping horse and had yet to notice the coming of dusk.

Faust Takes a Long Day's Journey through the Looking Glass with Madame Bovary

Fletcher Dunford worked in an East Side branch of the New York Public Library where he was walled in by books from floor to ceiling, which made him yearn to break out, run home, and write one himself. Each night he struggled with the same story whose sentences, despite the strength and forcefulness he tried to give them, never did march in step or pull together. Occasionally an entire paragraph would enchant him and later betray him as he glanced at it again the next morning when it read like a direct translation from the German. Often he would shout at the mirror, "You are a talentless dick." Sometimes he tried encouragement: "Listen, kid, if James Fenimore Cooper can do it, you can do it." Or a rousing battle cry: "Once more into the breach, dear friend, once more." Alas, in vain. So each morning he returned to his hardbound prison made up of millions of fine sentences woven into solid paragraphs and bound together into impressive volumes, trilogies sometimes, tetralogies even, while he could not manage to shackle together, to his own satisfaction, so much as three little words with the mystery and majesty of "Call me Ishmael."

He did not want success for the sake of wealth or to impress women. But to become a small part of what he loved most, that which had begun when he'd read, as a child, his first classic and had been amazed at how Dickens could summon, from dry print, all the comedy and calamity of life.

He'd first tried to be a writer in high school and at twenty-eight was still trying, but by then the keyboard of his computer seemed like the teeth of a great white coming at him through the deep. Even on Sunday his one-room apartment in East Harlem had the grim stillness of a torture chamber on the junta's day off. Was he never to know the pride and joy of being in print?

One dreary evening in spring, he took the crosstown bus to the comforting locale of his college days and ordered a beer in a bar he knew well on 114th Street, trying to forget about that great first line that would launch him into fiction and transform his vacant life.

Two beers later Billy Nutting came in, bought one for himself, and only then noticed his old friend Fletch, who stood up so they could hug each other. Billy hadn't changed. He still looked as if he dwelt in some happy place miles from maturity. They had met at Columbia, where Billy had seemed more a mascot than a student. Afterward, Billy had gone to California to further his computer training. Five years later, to the surprise of many, he'd returned in something like triumph, having been hired by a top communications firm. The word had gone out that he was brilliant, yet now, at twenty-six, he still seemed the same happy kid, without a worry in the world.

He had come all this way from Brooklyn to help a favorite professor of his who was having problems with his office computer. Then he'd made his way to this bar. They talked for a while about the classes they'd taken and the people they knew. Then Billy said, "You okay, Fletch? You seem low."

"That obvious, is it? Well, I'm fed up."

"Why? No, I insist. Tell me."

When Billy heard his old friend's tale of woe, he seemed delighted. "Fletch, you'll never believe this," and he explained that for a while now he had been working on a computer program designed to turn out quality advertising copy. Since he had made real progress at this, why not create software to write quality fiction? "Others are trying it. At the University of Dublin, for example. Really. The thing is to devise logarithms for all the known fictional tricks to see if digital storytelling can be, you know, summoned up. One needs, of course, a mega database of literary prose. I've always wanted to give it a shot, and now's my chance. It'll be exciting. Computers are literal beasts. Can we make them understand hyperbole and irony and whatever else they need? Anyway, a socko first sentence shouldn't be that hard to come by. Cheer up, Fletch, and let's get started."

The way forward was to find an excuse to use the lab where he worked when the others in the office had all gone home. This might be possible if they could enlist the aid of the owner's wife, who also worked there. Billy claimed to know her fairly well and said she was okay. A bit moody, but okay. No one would question them if she were there. And Billy had promised her free lessons in computer programming. It was the perfect setup.

Fletcher was excited, for this was better than that writing course that had taught him little or that how-to book from which he'd learned even less. Now the mighty computer would be his launching pad, and afterward he would forswear all digital magic and orbit on his own. Standing in the street, he forcefully shook Billy's limp hand on their joint Advanced Fiction Manufacturing Program.

Much work had to be done at the public library to assemble the brain matter to be uploaded into the mindless genius of Billy's office computer. But of course that week everything went wrong at work just when Fletcher needed peace and quiet. He had to chase up a delivery of new chairs that his branch manager had ordered but that hadn't arrived. The CD player for the children's weekly Reading Is Fun program broke down, Mrs. Flynn at checkout was home sick, and Fletcher, no lover of heights, again had to climb that creaking stepladder to replace a neon light.

Nevertheless, by staying after hours, Fletcher managed to collect all the punchy opening lines he had ever liked, starting with "O for a muse of fire." He did the same for final sentences, such as Faulkner's "Between grief and nothing, I shall take grief." Then he assembled dozens of lines that had made him shiver when he'd first read them. This, from James Joyce: "The heaventree of stars hung with humid nightblue fruit." Or Nabokov's sad evocation of a lost love: "Occasionally, in the middle of a conversation, her name would be mentioned, and she would run down the steps of a chance sentence, without turning her head."

Next he made a list of all the narrative forms he could think of: cyclical or linear, realistic or fantastic, comic or tragic, first person or third. He included the synopsis of a few overweight best sellers that were all plot and no story and added examples of those rare classics set purposely adrift in a nonnarrative sea: *Tristram Shandy* and *Malone Dies*. As Billy had requested, he assembled page upon page of assorted writing styles from Defoe to De Vries, from Henry James to Henry Miller, from James Joyce (early period) to James Joyce (middle period) to James Joyce (late period). Then, in nervous triumph, he dumped them all on Billy Nutting's desk for them to be melded into their program.

To do this, he rode an elevator up a tall glass building to the reception room of Magic Marketing Inc. with its hushed presence of discreet wealth. There were backless benches like marble coffins and a white-tiled floor the size of a skating rink. On the center wall was a vast painting of nothing in particular rendered with broad slaps of volcanic color as if the artist was furious with his own lack of inspiration.

Sitting in the crotch of a V-shaped desk was a young receptionist, arms bare, face grim. Fletcher sensed that if he came too close, he would become impaled on the many sharp aspects of her character.

It was as if she knew a hell of a lot about many things and what she knew greatly depressed her.

After he gave his name, she announced, through the intercom, that a Mr. Dunford was here to see William Nutting. Then she mumbled a glowering good night to a parade of happy employees escaping into the elevator. When she stood up and walked to the file cabinet, Fletcher, ever alert, noticed her figure.

"Nice day," he said.

She looked through the fortieth-floor window at the sludge-colored sky hanging low over the Hudson. "You're easily pleased."

"Let's start again. Been working here long?"

He feared his clumsy question would die in silence. After walking back and sitting down, she glanced up. "Put it this way. My earliest memory is sitting at this fucking desk."

He was saved from the harrowing prospect of further chitchat by the angelic appearance of Billy Nutting in a white coat. At the same moment, someone of obvious importance in his middle forties emerged from an office, his perfectly sculpted, prematurely bald head a living advert for the design capabilities of Magic Marketing. This energized Billy into rapid speech. "Though it's almost closing time, Mr. Dunford, do let me show you our setup." He quickly led his friend into the lab. When they had settled at a table by the coffee machine, Billy cautioned him that if anyone asked, they were working on a projection analysis involving venture-capital borrowing from German sources and that he should say he was from Morgan Chase to feed them data.

"Where's that wife you promised?" Fletcher asked, glancing around nervously.

"Speak of the devil," Billy whispered as the receptionist strode into the room. "Nina, this is Fletcher Dunford from," he said, giving her a wink, "Morgan Chase."

"You look like a banker the way Billy looks like Mike Tyson."

"Let's hope your husband doesn't see it that way," Fletcher said.

"No fear; his mind's on other things."

Billy brought her a chair, and they set to work force feeding Fletcher's research into the program. As Billy demonstrated the process, she made the occasional comment. "Nightblue fruit? That's weird." But when a security guard ambled by saying, "Hi, Nina," and she called back, "'Lo, Bruce," Fletcher saw how essential she was.

He thought feeding the machine would be easy. Perhaps it was. But the foreign language Billy used to teach Nina was beyond comprehension. It wasn't even a language. It was a top secret code, a perverse invention designed to exclude normal people from a private club of subversive nerds who alone understood a machine that from now on would simplify, accelerate, and plague Fletcher's life. He'd bought one some years ago but had never mastered the damned thing. It was similar to piloting a 747 jet of which 80 percent of its potential was a complete mystery to him, and so he taxied around on the tarmac, which suited his needs, not even learning how to take off.

Billy and his team worked three evenings a week, each session ending at ten o'clock. Then Nina headed home to her penthouse on East Eightieth Street to microwave a meal for her husband on his return from night school while her fellow conspirators relaxed at a bar down the street.

"She's attractive," Fletcher observed.

"He kept pestering her to marry him until she felt she had to quit her job or say yes. Now she hates him. He's great at marketing. Crap at everything else."

"I've noticed he doesn't even look at her."

Billy grinned. "Which is one thing we sure can't say about you."

"To be a good writer you have to observe stuff. Drink your beer."

The very next week the sleek bald head made a surprise appearance in the lab. Billy jumped up and introduced Mr. Dunford of Morgan Chase, explaining that they were working on a projection analysis involving venture-capital borrowing from German sources. Nina's husband seemed surprised and mildly pleased by Billy's initiative. He asked how things were down at Morgan Chase and

Fletcher shot back, "Finejustfine," as the laser eyes in that bald head peered into him like a jeweler skilled at finding flaws.

"And I'm getting free lessons in computer programming," Nina said in a self-satisfied tone.

Without looking at her: "So you told me." Then he left to attend, as he put it, "my mind-numbing night course in advanced economics." Nina made no comment, and, tactfully, neither did they.

Two days later Fletcher saw him in the lobby. The boss called out, "Hello, Morgan Chase," and got the reply, "Hello, Magic Marketing." They grinned and kept walking.

One night, Nina didn't rush off at ten o'clock. "I texted him to go microwave himself."

They all went for a drink, several in fact. She revealed something new, a wicked laugh that startled the room. But sometimes she stared at Fletcher as if amused for reasons he felt he was better off not knowing.

With his usual low-key good-bye, Billy made his way to Brooklyn. After watching him go, Nina said, "Come on, Fletch, I'll drive you home. It's in my direction."

"I'm further up town."

"Don't argue with the boss's wife."

While steering, smoking, and occasionally cursing at other cars, she said that Billy was a mystery to her. He didn't seem to have a love life or indeed any life to speak of. Perhaps she should fix him up with someone.

"Fletch, your girlfriend have a roommate?"

"Actually, I'm sort of, you know, between girls at the moment."

"Bugger. Now I've got to find someone for you too," she grumbled as she dropped him off in front of his building.

The next time they all had drinks she again drove him home, revealing how she yearned to run off and become an international airline hostess or a tour guide at the Hayden Planetarium or, bottom line, a lap dancer in Vegas. He, in turn, had to confess that his fantasy was to do all day just what he was doing now at night, typing alone in his room and, with any luck, adding to an ever-widening shelf in bookshops and libraries where the Dunford novels were kept.

"Really? Well, what kind of writer are you?"

"So far, alas, the kind who gains in translation."

"That's funny," she replied despondently.

When he climbed out of her car, he heard this: "By the way, I've found a girl for you."

"God almighty."

"My good deed for the day."

"Who is she?"

"Me," Nina said. He was too stunned to speak. "Well, sleep on it." She drove off.

Over the weekend he slept on it three times before he was able to see her again seated behind the prow of the desk.

"Did you mean it?" he asked.

She placed a yellow pad in the top drawer of her desk. "If the idea doesn't grab you, say so." With a salmon-pink fingernail, she slid a green paper clip past a marble penholder until it dropped soundlessly into the drawer. She shoved the drawer closed with a thump.

"Oh, it grabs me." He nodded several times. The absence of romance was harrowing.

"That's a yes, then, is it?"

"Three times a week," grumbled her bald husband, pausing at her desk, "and if that isn't enough, on Saturday I have to go on a field trip to Wall Street."

"All for the good of the firm," Nina said.

"Want to know my take on economics?" he asked no one in particular. "I think the clowns who teach it don't understand it themselves."

With a thumbs-up to Fletcher, he marched off, stopped, turned, and glanced at his wristwatch as the doors to the elevator closed.

Nina stared as if watching his slow descent to earth. "It took me years to find myself," she mused, "and when I did, guess what: I found myself married."

Billy appeared, all smiles. Their joint project was about to begin. In the lab, a few remaining odds and ends were fed into the memory bank. It was now programmed to the teeth. As would a pianist about to make his first entrance in a concerto, Billy's hands were poised above and then fell upon the keys to tap out instructions for it to produce that much-anticipated first line. A tiny ring kept circling, but nothing else appeared on the screen. Then came this:

> CALL ME ISHMAEL, AS STATELY, PLUMP BUCK MULLIGAN, MIDWAY IN LIFE'S JOURNEY, FOUR SCORE AND SEVEN YEARS AGO, WHEN ALL HAPPY FAMILIES WERE ALIKE, WENT DOWN TO THE PIRAEUS WHERE, IN THE BEGINNING, IT WAS THE BEST OF TIMES AND THE WORST OF TIMES EVER SINCE GOD CREATED THE HEAVENS AND THE EARTH.

Without waiting for anyone's comment, Billy deleted this and asked the machine to come up with something simple and better. This arrived:

WHEN I WAS JUNG AND AFREUD, I USED TO RIDE MY BISEXICLE.

Nina gave a dirty laugh. Billy, who hated puns, grimaced.

"The problem," Fletcher said, "is it has no story."

"Then give it one." Her hand clamped over her mouth, for she had spoken too loudly.

"Any ideas, Fletch?"

He couldn't think of a single plot line, not even the one of his own, so Nina took over. She said the story should start at the beginning of time and end at the present day. It should have a sympathetic central character and should be all about the pleasures of reading. She leaned back with a slight creative blush.

Before Fletcher could object, Billy said, "Let's give it a shot," and typed in her instructions. The little ring went round and round. Billy scratched his neck. Nina crossed her legs. Fletcher loosened his tie. A block of print filled the screen.

IN THE BEGINNING WAS THE BIG BANG. IT WAS SO VIOLENT GOD WAS HURT IN THE BLAST. HE WAS LEFT AN INVALID AND EVER SINCE HAS BEEN UNABLE TO CONTROL EARTHLY EVENTS. FOR MILLIONS OF YEARS HE WAS BORED, WITH NOTHING TO READ, JUST A FEW DEAD SEA SCROLLS AND THE FIRST HAND-PRINTED BIBLE, WHICH HE KNEW ALL ABOUT ANYWAY. WHAT HE WANTED WAS TO READ NOVELS AND PLENTY OF THEM. THERE WERE TWO PROBLEMS: (1) THE ALMIGHTY COULD FINISH A NOVEL IN SIX SECONDS, AND ALTHOUGH HE PREFERRED GREAT LITERATURE TO PURE PULP, THERE WOULD HAVE TO BE A VAST NUMBER OF BOTH TO KEEP HIM BUSY, AND (2) NOVELS DIDN'T EXIST YET. BUT HE KNEW THEY WERE COMING. HE WAS NO LONGER OMNIPOTENT, BUT HE WAS STILL OMNISCIENT AND COULD SEE WHAT LAY AHEAD. UNLESS HE DID SOMETHING, NOVELS WOULD NOT FLOURISH, AND HUMANS WOULD GET HOOKED ON POP MUSIC, TALK SHOWS, QUIZ SHOWS, COMPUTER GAMES, BOX SETS, AND ALL MANNER OF SPORTS. WHAT HE WANTED WAS TO MAKE THE BOOK INDUSTRY RIVAL THE OIL INDUSTRY OR AT LEAST THE FILM INDUSTRY SO THAT NOVELISTS WOULD PROLIFERATE. MANKIND WOULD BE UPLIFTED, AND GOD IN HIS HEAVEN WOULD HAVE PLENTY TO READ. HE SENT FORTH SAMUEL RICHARDSON, ALEXANDER DUMAS, WALTER SCOTT, HONORÉ DE BALZAC, GEORGE ELIOT, CHARLES DICKENS, MARCEL PROUST,

GEORGE SIMENON, AND MANY, MANY MORE. HE KEPT SENDING OTHER SUCH SAVIORS BECAUSE, SUCCESSFUL AS THEY WERE IN THE SHORT TERM, THEY EACH FAILED TO CONVERT HUMANITY TO THE TRUE WAY. SADLY, OF THE BILLIONS OF PEOPLE ON EARTH, FEW PAID ANY ATTENTION TO THESE LITERARY MIRACLE WORKERS. SO GOD DECIDED TO TRY ONE MORE TIME, AND HE SENT TO EARTH ISAAC ASIMOV WHOSE TASK WAS TO PRODUCE A FLOOD OF SCIENCE FICTION THAT WOULD NOT ONLY ENTERTAIN THE SUPREME BEING AND MAKE BOOK SALES SKYROCKET, BUT ALSO CREATE IN MAN THE URGE TO EXPLORE OUTER SPACE, POPULATE OTHER PLANETS, AND SPREAD THROUGHOUT THE UNIVERSE THE GOSPEL OF FICTION.

No one spoke for a moment. "Jesus," Nina said.

"Bit over the top, isn't it?" Billy asked.

But Fletcher whispered, "Fantastic." And he, among them, was the final arbiter of literary taste. His one concern was the story had no ending. Billy requested one. The computer complied.

This was the gist: Asimov, though more prolific than any fiction writer who ever lived, did no better than the others. Then God noticed in Manhattan a lazy writer trying, with the help of two friends, to machine-manufacture a story in the hope that technology would be the making of him. God saw the wider possibilities and gave the project His blessing. Of course the lazy writer would have to sit down and flesh out the finished product. But soon the machine might download not just stories but whole novels, trilogies sometimes, tetralogies even. And this would have come to pass except that one of those three apostles of the computer would prove to be a Judas, and the betrayal would ruin everything, especially for God.

Billy went pale. Nina's mouth hung open. Fletcher's scalp was wet. They found themselves standing and sat down again.

"Is this a practical joke?" Fletcher asked.

"Are you kidding, Fletch? Why would I?" Billy was too shaken to be doubted.

"It's enough to make you believe in God," Nina said.

"Or a computer virus," Fletcher added.

Billy was driven to make a personal statement. "I believe in technology. It is my life. That's why I use computers. I also accept coincidence, luck, and things mystical. That's how mankind deals with events for which we have no explanation and how we scientists deal with the bizarre without having to change our entire belief system. Follow me? So let us swear that we in this room are not now nor will ever be a Judas."

"Amen to that," Nina said.

"And let's not get sidetracked," Fletcher insisted. "Ask it for an opening line, one that fits the story this time. Then I'm out of here."

Billy typed, and the machine replied.

IN THE BEGINNING, GOD BIT OFF MORE THAN HE COULD CHEW.

"That's it." Fletcher stood up. "Finished. Now remember," he whispered, "if we stick together, we've got it made."

In the bar, Nina got real. "Profits shared three ways, agreed?"

Billy looked tired. "Come on, before we divvy up the proceeds, Fletch first has to write the damn thing."

They drank soberly. Then Billy patted his old friend on the shoulder, kissed the forehead of his boss's wife, and left for Brooklyn.

Nina, who had been badly shaken, now felt, after a few drinks, that she was okay to drive. When she stopped in front of his building, she alarmed him by killing the engine. His heart jogged in place. She got out. So did he. The lack of romance was still harrowing.

"We only have an hour," she warned as they climbed the stairs.

He hoped to have a chat first. There wasn't time, she said. He offered her a drink. No thanks. A lit candle in the darkened room was a desperate attempt to put himself in the mood. He doubted she would have cared had he used Klieg lights. She removed her clothes as if she were alone at home. Standing in the orange aura of that tiny flame, Nina nude seemed an artwork in a museum roped off from the viewer's reach. Then she leaped on him. In bed it was bliss. Apparently she agreed, for when she was dressed again, she offered him the soppy smile a loving mother gives to her priceless child, unremarkable as he may be. "Bye for now." And her high heels hurried down the stairs.

It took two weeks to write the story. It might have been finished sooner, except at lunchtime, on the very first day, he heard a light tapping at his door, and when he opened it, there stood Nina. She saw, she conquered, she came. What could be better than such an unexpected delight? Well, getting his work done, for a start. Yet he could hardly wait for her next interruption of his daily task of giving mouth-to-mouth resuscitation to his deathless prose. He wanted her, was mad for her, but would have preferred a somewhat-different her: gentle, sensitive, and moderate. Yes, that was it, moderate. Except when in his arms, of course. Why the devil was life so complicated?

When he got stuck for a good sentence to bring the story to an end, he went back to the Magic Marketing reception room, bantered with her bald husband, and followed a sour Nina into the lab. Billy, a bit subdued, conveyed his friend's request for a good closing line. The machine gave them its best shot.

> BETWEEN GRIEF AND NOTHING I SHALL TAKE GRIEF, WHICH IS A FAR, FAR BETTER THING THAN PUTTING HUMPTY DUMPTY BACK TOGETHER AGAIN, WHILE THE REST IS SILENCE, QUOTE THE RAVEN "NEVERMORE."

Fletch vetoed this cockamamie curtain line and asked instead for one fine punchy sentence, with compassion and insight, appropriate to the story the computer had invented. After a tense pause came the following:

> BUT THE POOR COMPUTER, WHO UPON REQUEST HAD CONJURED UP SUCH MAGIC THAT MAKES A STORY IMMORTAL, WAS NEVER PRAISED FOR HER LABOR NOR LOVED FOR HERSELF ALONE.

"I can relate to that," Nina said.

Fletcher was pleased to be handed such a good closing line. The computer hadn't said how the parable should end or who among them should be Judas, for which he was grateful, for he didn't want the monster to do everything. In his version, the rose-cheeked computer expert becomes jealous and tells his varnished-headed boss that his shapely wife has been sleeping with the man from Chase. When the husband learns he's been a cuckold, it hardly bothers him. But the rape, as he sees it, of one of his private computers sends him into a fury, and he takes hold of his computer expert and beats him to death with his wife's marble penholder.

Delighted with his story, Fletcher showed it to Nina, who liked it but wondered if anyone else would. Might this be a case of never have so many written so much for so few? But he was undeterred and, the next morning, sent it off to a magazine whose editor was an old acquaintance from some years back. Perhaps this would get him a quick reading.

Now, though, his day job seemed more depressing than ever. Mrs. Flynn was home ill again, two of their five free computers were down, thefts of books were up this month, and would you believe it? Another neon light was flickering.

Finally, some rare good luck freed him from the suspense of waiting to learn whether he would ever be a writer. His branch manager asked him to go to Vermont for two weeks to catalogue a house full of books. An old lady had left them in her will to this very library where, decades ago, she had spent many a happy hour. Her daughter, who lived nearby, said there would be a small bedroom for Fletcher to sleep in. Otherwise the house would be empty, and he would be left alone to get on with the job.

Nina asked if she could come with him. It would be fun. She would tell her husband that she had to attend to a sick friend. And she knew someone who would gladly sit in as receptionist. It would be very cozy together in Vermont. She could even help out with the work he had to do. He felt a jab of fear as when a window appeared on his laptop warning, DANGER, THIS ACTION CANNOT BE PERFORMED SAFELY. Not having her near him was irksome. Yet the thought of this strong-willed woman sharing his bed every night and helping to catalogue books every day was oppressive, its outcome unpredictable. He wanted nothing to go wrong between them, and such closeness threatened collision. Sadly he gave her his answer. No. He would work faster alone. *No?* Her face winced with pain.

"You don't want me."

"I do want you, and when I return, we'll really get to know each other, slowly and properly."

She stared at him with that unseeing, all-knowing look. Then she changed tack and ordered him to go and work his ass off. "And I hope you're lonely as hell." As her high heels hammered down the stairs, he felt utterly bereft.

The old lady's house was a short walk uphill from the train station. The floor of her library creaked like crickets. Many of the books were classics, some even leather bound with three volumes of color reproductions of the great Dutch painters. On her kitchen table, oddly enough, was a paperback by Asimov. The bedroom that had been made ready for him contained several teddy bears, Winnie the Pooh curtains, and photos of male rock stars. The local grocery store satisfied most of his needs. He worked hard as memories of Nina kept slithering into the house. One night he heard her tapping softly on his bedroom door. He opened it twice and on neither occasion, in his dream or afterward when he awoke, was she there. Whenever he tried her cell phone, it was turned off, so he sent a text: "You are in my heart." No reply. When he phoned the office, she sounded depressed, said she couldn't talk, and put him through to Billy: "Hey, there, Fletch, how's Vermont?" He e-mailed saying how much he missed her. No reply.

When the job was done and he returned home, a letter was waiting. His story had been accepted. Not bothering to unpack, he hurried to that glistening glass structure, took the elevator to Magic Marketing Inc., and ran to the v-shaped desk to fling his good news down in front of her. It was six in the evening, and she was gone. A button on her phone winked at him slyly. Well, he would tell Billy, for it was his victory too. Then Nina's husband emerged from the inner office in a terrible state. Seeing Fletcher, he broke down and had to be helped onto a marble bench.

"I made Billy Nutting. Gave him his big break. What does he do? I'll tell you what he does. He skips out with my wife to LA. Oh, that slimy bastard. Can I borrow your handkerchief?"

Fletcher walked home through a bleak city where no one in the rush-hour crowd noticed his tears. When he got back, he checked his e-mails, and there it was.

Hi Fletch,

Sitting with Billy one evening in the bar after work he seemed low. Was it his love life? He just shrugged. Look, I told him, you just haven't found the right girl yet. Pick some nice consenting adulteress and give it a try. Not even a smile. Come on, I said, I'll drive you home. Well, by now you probably know what happened. I was angry at you, and I was angry at my husband, and Billy is always so sweet. Can you believe it? I suddenly became the older woman teaching a young lad about life. It went well. A few more lessons, I thought, and he'll be ready to solo. That's not the word I'm looking for, but you know what I mean.

Then amazingly he gets this great job offer from LA and asks would I like to come with him? Just like that. No big deal. I said, you bet your sweet ass I would.

We instructed the black monster to write my farewell note to heartless hubby. This, I swear, is what popped up. Between grief and Nutting, i will take Nutting. No, I didn't use it. Although the pompous fathead deserves that and more. He just wanted me around when it suited him. Like you did. Oh, Fletch, things could have been so different. Well, that's that, I guess.

We both hope your computer story sees the light of day. OK, maybe I betrayed you but you betrayed yourself. Which is worse? You tell me.

Good-bye then. Billy sends his best and says he's sorry. All he did was cherish me when I needed it. Fletch, I will always remember you. In fact just yesterday your name was mentioned, and you ran down the steps of a chance sentence, and we waved.

COME LIVE WITH ME
AND BE MY LOVE

She was desperate to escape from London because her turbulent affair with a member of Parliament had come to a painful end. Luckily, the publishing house Ginda worked for, Bellamy & Donate, had an opening in their New York office, and soon she found herself on the Upper West Side in a tall city filled with bizarre surprises. For example, the apartment her office had arranged for her to live in came furnished with a man. Everyone at the publishing house assured her that this sort of thing often happened in Manhattan due to a need to share the frightening rent.

The man's name was Mickey Travis, and he also worked at Bellamy & Donate. He had been eager to find someone because the woman whose job Ginda was taking and whose bed she would be sleeping in had left for Chicago to join her lover. Sharing with Mickey would be safe, she was told, for who would misbehave when she could just walk out, leaving him like Atlas bent under that appalling financial burden?

Mickey was a line editor with a face like a first draft. He talked nervously about his work, his diet, his jogging. And he had an odd habit of speech. When he first ushered her into the living room or handed her a cup of tea or gave her a receipt for the first month's rent, each time he said, "There you go." She was safe, no question. This man was sweet, timid, and unattractive. And so forty-eight hours after she left Heathrow, she had settled in and gone to work. *Things do happen quickly here,* she thought. Two weeks later she was in love.

Ginda was beginning to get her footing in this city of obsessive commerce and manic nightlife when she was assigned a manuscript by an actor with the doctored name of Sky Brady. He had been with a touring company in China performing plays in English. His journal of this experience gripped her, and she recommended it for publication. The chief editor was doubtful until, on that very weekend, a book on China by a rival house climbed onto the best-seller list.

Mickey Travis, to tease Ginda, referred to her new author as the Skywriter. She went along with the joke until she met with Brady to discuss his manuscript. There was already no question in her mind that he was a born writer. Now there was no question that he was a born actor. His mobile face was lean, intense, expressive, and, at rest, wonderfully arresting. His dark hair splashed about with dramatic effect, and his sudden smile filled her with awe.

He arranged for a ticket to be left for her at the box office so she could admire him in a small part in an off-Broadway play soon to close. He had two speaking lines but did some insolent slouching, snatched some money from an old lady, disappeared, and didn't return until it was time for his bow.

Since she was new to the city, he became her guide to "his" New York, showing her where he'd gone to high school, then drama school, and finally pointing out a number of shabby buildings where he'd once lived. He recited poems to her in a probing voice deep as a cello. She marveled at how he managed to be more fascinating than interesting. Whenever they met, they talked about what they always talked about when they met: him. Still, his vivacious self-absorption was intriguing. It was as if he had discovered finally the purpose of life, which was to bring to as many as possible the rare gift of Sky Brady. Then one night he kissed her. It took place at two in the morning at the top of some wet subway steps that had just been hosed down with strong detergent.

Soon he won another off-Broadway role in a drama about a South American revolution. He was to share the stage with, among others, a young Hispanic actor who Sky said was superb. His name, Raoul. He wore sandals and dark glasses.

She spent hours in Sky's apartment helping him memorize his lines while on the neighboring roof pigeons cleared their throats. It was during one of these sessions that they first went to bed. Afterward, she knew she wanted to be with him always and to live with him now.

This new love became a treacherous sea, and just one person could keep her afloat if only he could be distracted from his own life to be more aware of hers. And Sky did make room for her in his busy existence. He was warmed by her devotion, enamored by her love. So she did seem to be getting through to him, moving from the margin of his life to that all-important place close to the center of his career. As he sought an audience of millions, she would be able at least to seat herself in the very front row.

His life was chaos, and she tried to arrange it like a table setting. Since he never cleaned his room, twice a month she did it for him. He seemed more touched by this than anything else she did. One day, with great ceremony, he took out a small gift-wrapped box tied with a blue ribbon. She unwrapped it, trying to keep calm. It was a key to his flat.

On opening night she couldn't eat. She sat nervously in the audience as he walked on stage in a flood of light like God in an opened-neck shirt. She expected magic. All she saw was Sky Brady attempting to be someone other than her lover. Was he a good actor? The critics didn't help. Some faintly praised him; some didn't notice him at all. Raoul, on the other hand, seemed born into the drama as if he had no other existence.

Ginda had a logistics problem. How did a nine-to-five working girl manage a love affair with someone who slept until noon, had to be at the theater at seven, and got off again at a quarter to eleven? More than once she spent her lunch hour napping at her desk.

For his birthday she bought him a three-sided mirror for his dressing table. When he was busy performing at a Wednesday matinee, she took the day off, hailed a taxi, and afterward carried the great bloody bulk of this gift step by step up the four flights to his poky room. She left it in the hall, got out the key, and went in to clear some space on his table.

Sky was in bed with Raoul. Black hair shrouded her lover's face. With a toss of his head he revealed a beleaguered expression quickly changing to something like pride. She stood wordless, useless. The room was an oven.

"It's Wednesday," she whispered.

"It's Thursday," he corrected. A passing truck rattled the windows. "What do you want?" he asked.

The skin of his body was as white as winter. The other one was tan with the season's licentiousness. A pair of jeans lay on the floor, one leg pulled inside out. A hundred years passed. "Your birthday present," she said, her eyes closed, "is in the hall."

She had no memory of leaving. A woman in the street asked if she was okay. At a pay phone she found she was still holding his key. It chimed in the gutter, a last fragment of happiness. She dialed and asked for Mickey Travis, please, like a normal person, and caught him as he was leaving for lunch. The plan was to inform him calmly of the death of her life, then gulp down the sedative of his concern. He had always listened to her woes. But now she couldn't speak. Her face changed shape as if a great force were trying to pull it apart. He kept calling her name. "'S'me," she finally squeaked, became blinded, and fled. She walked all the way home. Mickey was there in the street, waiting. She gave a fraudulent smile for the doorman, but when they were safely upstairs, she fell apart, appalled by her shameless grief. Oh, how ugly she must look.

He made her coffee. "There you go," he said, frightened yet willing to supply whatever she needed except the hug he didn't know she yearned for as he sat beside her. When she told him what had happened, it was her turn to be frightened. He rose and slapped the wall. Shouted at the ceiling. He would tear Sky Brady apart. She had no idea he had become that fond of her. He was a tall blur on the far side of her tears as he made for the door. She must stop him. Yet how forceful he was. She ran to the stairwell. From below came the cantering dance of his hurried descent.

"Mickey, for God's sake, he's one of our authors."

She dialed Sky's number. Busy signal. A taxi took her to the phone booth where she had thrown his key away. Found it. His birthday present was still in the hall. The door was partly open. He was sitting on the floor holding the bedsheet to his right eye, his nose bleeding.

"Do I look awful?" he asked, wincing in pain. "He told me not to see you again, ever. I refused, and he hit—ow—hit me."

"Poor you," Ginda said.

"How do I look?"

"Lovely. Just different."

She nursed him with a sandwich bag of crushed ice, and though he was frail with pain, she took him, at his insistence, to the theater. The others were shocked, but he refused to say how it had happened. Raoul made him wear a hat to shield the damage. Standing in the wings, he needed her to steady him. She didn't know how he got through the evening, and when he took a bow, she was sobbing.

The real Theatre of the Absurd takes place backstage, she realized. He was hugged and deified while he made light of a triumph he was all but milking to death. Ginda slipped away into the dark street.

She now saw her flat mate anew. He was brave and forceful and not at all safe to live with. She hailed a taxi and climbed in as Sky Brady came running. He wanted her to stay with him, to live with him. Standing at the open window, he was in tears. "I will never see him again." When she gave the driver her address, Sky said, "I'm going to dedicate the book to you."

"Me? Not Raoul?"

"Raoul? After what he did to my face? Are you kidding?"

By the time she got home her newfound hero had dwindled again into a roommate. He climbed out of his chair and turned off the TV.

"I got to his place but didn't go up."

"I see."

"Didn't want to be a brute and lower myself in your esteem."

"Ah."

"You all right?"

"Yop."

"Now that it's over," he said, "I thought we might—you and I might …"

"You're very sweet, Mickey. But, to be honest, I just don't …"

"Right," he said. "Understood."

"Really knackered. I'm off to bed, I'm afraid."

"Sure."

But sleep didn't come. "Bugger this." She got up and slipped a note under his door. It said, "Shall I cook dinner for us tonight?" Back in bed, she smiled as she imagined placing a dish of pasta in front of him, saying, "There you go." She could not avoid reliving the high farce of her bruising day off. Well, another lesson learned. Then she banished all that to cherish the note awaiting him on the floor in his room. After a deep breath and another she banished even that and slept.

IF MUSIC BE THE FOOD OF LOVE

The most bizarre character I ever met, outside my immediate family, was also the worst teacher I ever had. And in those days there was no lack of competition.

For example, Mrs. Mctavish, who taught biology, held the view that repetition was the key to learning, and so the entire class found itself chanting such simple truths as "Egg plus sperm equals fertilized egg; egg plus sperm equals fertilized egg." Mr. Lebeau, our French instructor, purposely made screeching sounds with blackboard chalk, and when we all groaned, he held up his hand, the middle finger bent out of sight, and said, "What are you complaining about? Look what happened to me." Economics was taught by "Mr. What," so nicknamed due to his constant questions. "Bad money drives out what? The direction of a bull market is what? Inflation is what? Depression is what?" Soon "What? What? What?" was all we heard. And Mr. Rickman, our gym teacher, advised the boys in hygiene class that if we ever met up with a "fairy," we were to put things right by giving him a severe beating.

We had no opinion of our school principal. His lofty position elevated him far above the basic tasks of education. Rarely seen in the halls, he dwelt in a large room with a desktop as polished as a ballroom floor. Within arm's reach was a microphone into which he occasionally made solemn pronouncements that were broadcast with biblical portentousness throughout the school. "This is Mr.

Tinworth. I would like to speak to you this morning on the proper way to salute your country's flag."

Hillside High School was simply a place we were forced to inhabit until the last bell set us free. Yet there was one class I couldn't wait to attend. On the top floor, in room 305, Mr. Itzkowitz taught a class called Enjoying Classical Music, and his lucky students, I was told, listened to Toscanini conducting Beethoven and Beecham doing Mozart. Itzkowitz also compared renditions by various pianists as they played Schubert, Chopin, and Brahms.

To me, an only child, classical music was like having an assortment of dear friends. Tchaikovsky and Schubert and I went back for so many years I couldn't remember when we first met. Much later, I discovered that the first two records my father owned were the *Pathétique* and *Death and the Maiden*, which he'd played over and over while I'd crawled about on the living room floor. Chopin soon became an intimate, while Dvorak never failed to cheer me up. Bach withheld his great secret until I went to high school. But Beethoven was the very model of manhood, while Brahms offered autumnal wisdom. Haydn was weighty, witty, and indispensable. Mozart, who at first seemed quaint, slowly rose to almost unbearable perfection.

So I walked into my first music class as into a cathedral. I was ready. I was never more ready. It was then I discovered that the legendary Mr. Itzkowitz was no longer with us (he had been snapped up by a private school and carried off to Boston), and in his place stood a Mr. E. Trundle, whom none of us had ever seen before. His bald head had a semicircular fringe of hair that stood up like grass. He wore a Hitler mustache and Heinrich Himmler glasses and, when he smiled, displayed a gap-toothed grimace perfect for a horror film.

The students filed in quietly, trying to get the measure of the man. It didn't take long. One of the last to enter was Francene Swick, who brightened my life whenever she appeared. She was forever exuding goodwill in generous smiles. I knew well her soundless laugh, that head toss of blonde hair, her blight of braces over which her beauty triumphed. I soon learned how absorbed she was in music, totally unaware of how absorbed I was in her. It wasn't that she eclipsed the other girls. It was more like what other girls?

Mr. Trundle stood up, adjusted his glasses, introduced himself, and said, "Welcome. I hope in time we will really get to know each other. But now we must move right along because we have a lot of ground to cover. Today we will study music by a man some consider the greatest composer who ever lived. The three Rasoumovsky quartets, or Razumoffsky, as it is sometimes spelled." He wrote this out on the blackboard. "Or 'ovsky' or even 'owsky.'" He wrote them out too. Before he turned to face us, a paper glider, thrown at Francene Swick, third row, fourth seat, dove into the open desk of "Fat" Biggs, seated next to her, which he closed and leaned on, none the wiser. "The three Rasoumovsky quartets were composed by Ludwig van Beethoven and dedicated to Count Rasoumovsky, the Russian ambassador in Vienna, who was a keen quartet player himself." Trundle clasped his hands behind his back and rocked on his heels. "They are among the most noble creations in the pantheon of great chamber music, and we will explore them together today and for the next several weeks."

It was not to be.

"Rats are what?" asked Pete Castilano.

"Rats are muffsky," someone shouted from the rear, evoking poisonous laughter.

Mr. Trundle looked as if he had been slapped. He then panicked, announcing a demerit for "The boy in seat 7D—no, 7C—no, I mean 8C" as he indicated to a girl, who had been assigned to check the attendance with the class chart, that she should here and now enter this punishment into the ledger.

It was like firing demerits at Attila the Hun.

"Aw, I want a demerit too," some lout protested.

"Me too, Teach."

A disapproving "Tsh" came from Francene, who, to my delight, also wanted this music to be appreciated, not desecrated. I caught her eye, something I had never been able to do before, and we shook our heads in mutual despair. I was thrilled.

Mr. Trundle looked much as the captain must have when he first understood that the *Titanic* was doomed. Then, in desperation and with a good deal of foot stamping and ugly bellowing, the class was finally subdued. Clearing his throat, a careful Mr. Trundle stepped ever so gingerly into the breach.

"A quartet is any of four performers, vocal or instrumental. A piano quartet, for example, is a piano joined with three stringed instruments. Joseph Haydn, born in 1732, invented the symphony and also the string quartet. Indeed, he invented chamber music as we know it."

Francene scribbled notes, her shining hair guarding the page from wayward glances, while I kept an eye on our teacher as I would on an inexperienced member of a bomb-disposal team. Our room on the top floor overlooking the playing field had one of its three windows open. Trundle ceased talking and looked horrified. Louie Bruno was crouched on the sill. "Good-bye, world, I'm gonna end it all." He jumped into space. Trundle screamed, and Bruno fell the entire two feet to the balcony below. An explosion of laughter. Trundle engaged in yet more bellowing and foot stamping until the door flew open and in burst Mr. Rickman as if hot on the trail of fairies.

"What's going on here?" he boomed like the top sergeant he once was. The class went as cold as a corpse. "Bruno, what in devil's hell are you doing outside that window?"

"Fell, sir."

"Then you must be even more stupid than I thought. Get your ass in here. The noise of this … this zoo … can be heard all the way across the hall. If I have to come in here again, I'm banging heads, do you read me?"

The room became void of sound. An ominous breeze chilled us. Then Mr. Rickman departed behind a slammed door. Not once had he looked at Mr. Trundle, who stood there as chastised as the rest of us. He blinked. Adjusted his glasses. I thought he might cry.

Instead he put a record on the Victrola and wound the crank. He said he would introduce us first to the slow movement of I forget which Rasoumovsky. We listened. A heartrending meditation swelled softly into that barbaric room. Francene and I and the traumatized Mr. Trundle were drawn into another place.

"It is enough to make one cry," he had said before allowing the fat silver arm to rest on the turning record with its rotating dog on its rotating label. And sure enough Pete Castilano was rubbing his fist into his eye, and soon "Fat" Biggs, hands over face, was shaking in misery, and Louie Bruno had his hankie out and began sobbing audibly while several of the other guys were rocking as if at the Wailing Wall. Mr. Trundle killed the music and burst out with, "5F—no, 6F—I mean 7G—and you too, 3E—no, I mean F, yes, 3F and also ..."

When the bell rang, Mr. Trundle said, "Now, class, please listen, class, because next Tuesday I want you all to consider ..." But the room had already emptied as if at the start of a cross-country run. Mr. Trundle did nothing. He just stared into those awful rows of vacant seats.

"I just loved the Beethoven," Francene said, like someone who had flown in on white wings to make an annunciation.

He looked wildly at her as if, desperate for something kind to say, she had praised his underwear.

As I left the room, trying not to think of what had happened and, worse, would continue to happen, I rested my eyes on her bouncing hair and the sheathed metronome of her hips as she carried her books down the hall. Then she halted, turned, spoke.

"Isn't it terrible, what they're doing?"

"Yes, terrible."

"Someone should stop them."

"Someone should."

"Those awful, awful boys."

"Awful."

"I'm glad you agree."

She shook her head and walked off, leaving me with a dry throat and a resolution to improve my conversational skills.

But next week Francene was absent, the class a disaster, Mr. Trundle once more transformed into a fool. I was depressed for the rest of the day. The following Tuesday Francene swept back in looking more lovely than I had remembered and gave me a lingering smile, having no idea, I'm sure, what that could do to some poor lad stretched out on the rack of youth. Once more Mr. Rickman burst in and kicked ass while Mr. Trundle seemed to shrink as if hoping his entire life would go away and a far, far better one would take its place.

When the class ended and Mr. Trundle had fled, a few of the ringleaders stayed behind, drawn to the persistent mystery of Francene's snuggly clothed body.

"Why don't you behave yourselves?" she scolded, deciding to confront them at last. Louie Bruno knocked her books from under her arm, and Pete Castilano stole her pen when it rolled away. As she sought to retrieve it, trying not to seem angry, he tossed it to "Fat" Biggs, and when she approached him, he lobbed it to someone else.

As I tried to put a stop to this substitution for a gang bang, Castilano wrestled me to the floor from behind while Bruno pulled off my left shoe and tossed this around as well. Francene, coming to my aid, called out, "Stop that!" and, after giving a yelp, shouted, *"You take your hands off me!"* when someone pinched her rump.

Now the door burst open to the almighty shout of *"What in hell's going on in here?"*

Pete Bruno pointed at me and said, "He's hitting us with his shoe."

Mr. Rickman took most accusations at face value for it greatly simplified things, particularly if one refused to listen to a second opinion as he refused now to listen to Francene's. So he pronounced me guilty and, in a loud voice, ordered me on detention.

This meant that for one week I had to get up at seven, when it was creepy dark, instead of eight, when healthy sunlight was everywhere. I had to rush to school at 7:55, instead of ambling in just this side of nine. Once there I was expected to sit and study in the empty auditorium—empty except in the back where could be found that little knot of boys who were well on their way to becoming tomorrow's drunks, felons, and muggers. That month, a sour-faced Mr. Hellerstein, who taught history, had the assignment of guarding these early-hour inmates and seeing to it that they didn't slide even further into trouble. Often, he stepped out into the hall to sneak a smoke, stepped back to peer at us, his hand behind his back, then furtively disappeared again trailing a cloud of white vapor.

It was a grim thing, detention. We slumped in our seats, yawning and disgruntled, or sat bent over our unyielding school books or, like the boy next to me, sketched on a note pad an assortment of buxom babes. Then it happened.

Far away and at the very bottom of the auditorium, a door opened, and in came a small man who walked as though hoping to be unobserved. He stopped, stooped, opened the lid to bare the piano's teeth, sat, paused, and played. In Mr. Trundle's hands the grand piano filled every inch of that vast place with first one and then another and finally all of Chopin's preludes.

He had a delicacy of touch that filled the music with painful slivers of bliss. There was thoughtful sadness, restrained exultation, and then those splendid, devilish, final bass notes of doom.

Silence.

Mr. Trundle stood, stooped, closed the mouth on those gleaming teeth, and walked off.

When he had begun to play, the prisoners in the back rows had looked up, then down again in boredom. Mr. Hellerstein had glanced over at the pianist, looked back at his prisoners, and slipped out into the hall. I couldn't believe my luck. When I returned the next morning, Mr. Trundle reappeared to fill the place with Brahms. On Wednesday there was an hour of angry Beethoven. Next, Debussy, with his sunken cathedrals and reflections in water. And on Friday, which was, sadly, my last day of punishment, I was treated to Scarlatti, Clementi, Shubert and Liszt.

Just think, I had only to be bad again to enjoy five more such mornings. The only trouble was every Tuesday afternoon I would have to watch another forty-five minutes of his heartrending humiliation. I wanted to apologize for his pain, to agitate for his salvation. But all I did was go to my next class and conjugate the verb "to be."

Ten minutes later, Mr. Lebeau chose me, out of all the others in French class, to deliver an envelope to Mr. Rickman. At first I felt fortunate to be free of French. As I made my way into the depths of the building, toward my destination, I passed the echo chamber of the gymnasium where came a voice I recognized all too well. Poor Mr. Trundle was rehearsing the orchestra.

It was a spirited ensemble of determined tunelessness, of rhythmic derangement. Sometimes they became a platoon of dentists drilling in unison; at other times, a musical vacuum where Vivaldi should have been. They would deliver a chorus of razor cuts, then a discernible tune, then not. It was Vivaldi, all right, but with Alban Berg struggling to get out.

Mr. Trundle conducted and shouted and stamped and conducted. I stood with my head against the wall, grimacing. I managed to stay there until the bell brought an end to the nightmare. Then came healthy noises as the children fled from their calamity. I peeked in. The gym was empty. Four rows of chairs were empty. The boxed podium underneath the basketball hoop was empty. I walked to a door that led to the locker rooms.

He was seated on one of the long benches resting a leather-bound flask on his left knee. The fringe of his bald head was upswept, as usual, and his rimless glasses were like transparent growths on his face. His tie was loose, his lips open.

He saw me and swung the flask behind him.

"Ah," he cried, as if stabbed. Straightening slightly, "Yes? You forgot something?"

"I'm not in the orchestra, sir. Just … passing by."

"You wish to get to your locker, perhaps."

"No, sir."

"You don't?" This with mounting suspicion.

"I, well … I was in the auditorium all this week and heard you play."

He peered at me as if to ready himself for a new humiliation. "You were in detention, then. One of those boys." He glanced at the doorway for possible cohorts.

"Well, yes."

"Aha." I was clearly the enemy.

"No, but I just wanted to say how wonderful it was. The Chopin. Everything. Someday I'd love to hear you play the four ballades." Although a sophomore, I was trying hard not to be sophomoric. "And the Debussy was magical. At home we have records of Rubinstein and Serkin. I couldn't tell the difference. Between them and you, I mean. I just wanted you to know this."

He stood up and was at a loss for having done so. "Very kind. Very kind. What's that?"

I looked at the envelope in my hand. "Oh, this is for Mr. Rickman."

"You had better give it to him."

"Yes."

He was still holding his left hand behind his back. My praise seemed to have dropped into a void. I said good-bye, and he nodded, still puzzling over me.

"Were you ever a concert pianist?" I asked.

"Yes, well … no, not really. Wanted to be. But no." He shook his head.

"Why not? I mean, what happened?"

He looked away. "You see … it was a case of nerves." He looked back at me. "A bad case of nerves." He brightened. "Schnable was my teacher for a time."

"Was he really?"

"Oh yes. Had high hopes. Others too. A condition of the nervous system, it just … made it impossible, you see."

"I'm sorry."

"Oh well." He make light of it all with a gap-toothed smile. "Never mind. Gave it a try. Have my memories."

"Ah, right."

"Played for Arrau once, in Paris."

"Wow, did you?"

He stopped, as if ashamed by some indiscretion. I didn't know how to continue either.

"Well, thanks again," I said.

"No, I thank you."

After I left, I was cheered by the thought of seeing him in class next week. But by then he was gone from the school. Nothing was said, and music appreciation was discontinued until next term.

Francene Swick stunned me in the hall one day by speaking my name. Since we no longer shared a class, I hadn't seen her in weeks. Her braces were gone. She seemed to have acquired a new mouth, erotic and ready, bracketed as it had been with those charming character lines in those slightly sunken cheeks. Her eyes became enlarged as if to draw me into all that cornflower blue.

"He's gone. They drove him away."

"I know." And I managed to tell her of our talk in the locker room.

"Oh, that's good. Oh, I'm really glad you did that."

I swallowed and gave it a try. "Look, I'm thinking of asking Mr. Tinworth to give me Trundle's address. To write to him. We can both write to him. Together, I mean. Compose a letter after school, if that's okay. And both sign it."

She smiled. I was certain she could see right through this little proposal of mine right down to my boxer shorts. She spoke as through an erotic turbulence that let in the words but delayed their meaning.

"I'm taking typing lessons," she said. "If you come to my house, I can practice as we write it."

We agreed on a day. We agreed on a time. Here was a cue for a song. Her place, I said, was fine.

The "late" bell rang through the empty halls. She touched my arm and hurried off, her hips in jaunty four-four time.

When the last class that day ended, I went to the principal's office and carefully knocked. Told to enter, I stepped in a large room where, at its center, was a polished desk with a microphone of gleaming silver. Mr. Tinworth, well dressed and with a dark mustache, stood by an open file cabinet as if posing for his picture. He gave me a disapproving "Yes?"

My mumbled request tumbled out. Mr. Tinworth closed the cabinet and turned to face me. He had an actor's voice.

"That is kind and thoughtful. I will take note and notify your homeroom teacher of your concern. I will do the same for Miss Swick."

I waited. He waited. It was warm in there. He pulled slightly at each white shirt cuff of his dark-blue double-breasted suit.

"I regret I must inform you that Mr. Trundle passed away last week."

Laughter rose up to us from the front steps of the school.

"How? What happened?"

"It is inappropriate for me to say more than what I have already said."

"Did he kill himself?"

"These private matters are no concern of yours."

"He did, didn't he?"

"Did you hear what I just said, young man? Remember to pray for him. Tell Miss Swick to pray as well. And please close the door when you leave."

A Feminine Ending

—Hi, this is Claude Shell. I just stepped out for a moment. If you're phoning to offer me a film contract or a part in a Broadway play, please do. But only after the bleep. (*Bleep*)

—Hello, Claude, this is Becky. What's happening, my love? Haven't heard from you in days. Are you angry? Are you unwell? One worries. One would like to hear from you. Phone one, okay? Lots of love. And all for you.

—Greetings, this is Claude Shell, the actor. Sorry, but I'm out at the moment fighting the forces of evil. If you're a stage producer or a movie mogul or even just a friend, leave your name, and I'll ring you, pronto. Let's hear it for the beautiful bleep. (*Bleep*)

—It's me again. I phoned two days ago. Reply there was none. Don't I even get an explanation? I cannot believe that you would do your Charlie Chaplin shuffle down the hall, stop, turn, blow me a kiss, leap into the elevator and out my life. Just like that. It's not fair. I really want to talk to you, Claude. I'm very depressed. Please have the courage to be courteous. I mean that. Okay? Bye for now.

—My fellow Americans, this is Ronald Reagan. I've just stepped out of office to go down in history. How far down, I can't say. But if you have a message for my favorite actor, Claude Shell, who was far better than I ever was, which is not saying much, begin at the bleep. (*Bleep*)

—I know you're there, Claude. You keep changing your intro. The Ron thing is good. Nice imitation. Very droll. Producers should love it. I'm sure they'll get a big bang out of you. But I can say from experience that a big bang doesn't drown out the primal scream. If you follow me. Look, I'm hurting. The longer the silence, the more the pain. I got back to work on my novel last night. Might as well since I'm home all the time waiting for your call. I have a title finally. *A Feminine Ending* by Rebecca Rasbatch. Hell, I don't want to work in a shop all my life. But it's slow. I mean, how am I expected to write high-gloss, nondrip prose while waiting for a phone call that never comes? Bad for the soul, ditto one's concentration. So be a good guy, and give us a call. Nudge, nudge. Love you, sweetie. Bye for now.

—Hi, this is the charismatic Becky Rasbatch, who is either hard at work at Electronics Plus on Seventh Avenue or out for the evening with some boring man. So leave your particulars, and I'll get back to you. Do not ask for whom the machine bleeps; it bleeps for thee. (*Bleep*)

—Okay, this is Claude. It's over. Okay? I'm sorry, but that's the way it is. Sorry. It's just that some things reach the end, and then they're over. Simple as that. Look, there are other men, other answering machines. Try one of them. Give me a break. You're a good kid. Very pretty, very funny. Everybody likes you. Okay? Lots of luck. Have a good life.

—Here is Gorbachev, premier of the Soviet Union and environs. H'm not here this moment. If you vish to reach me or my dear friend Comrade Claude Shell, that vunderful actor appearing all veek on TV in great Smirnoff commercial, then you leave please message now. At bleep. Vait, it vill come. If I tell it to come, it vill come. (*Bleep*)

—Oh, Claude. You rang me at home when you knew I'd be at work. How safe. No chance I'd embarrass you with all this sticky love I'm stuck with. That's just so typical. Why are you like this? No one can reach you, can they, Claude? Not even on the phone. But I know you're there. You just don't answer. You hide in the closet till the machine clicks off. And I'm the one who sold you the damned thing. I demonstrated all our machines, and you demonstrated all your charms. Even told Mr. Crimshaw what a lovely saleslady he had in his employ. Then I watched you cross the street to a phone booth, and suddenly there's a ringing in the store, and it's you asking for Miss Ras*butch*, which is how we had our first romantic lunch at McDonald's. Well, I know something others who phone you don't know: that the machine I sold you can record really long messages. This is because you don't want to miss a word some long-winded theater person might have to say to you, isn't that so, my sweet? So now poor you must listen to obsessed me until I finally hang up and let Steven Spielberg get through. Oh, Claude, I miss you so much. Tell me—who rubs your back now? Helps you memorize scripts? Lends you her makeup? When you walked out, you left behind something priceless—the unfinished story of our love. Now just unbound pages tumbling away in the wind. My scattered life blown asunder. Are you listening? Am I reaching you? Let me try again. We were woven together to make a single, solid tapestry. Now it's been torn apart. My half, a tattered rag. Sorry to be crying. Not on purpose. 'Cause I'm not. It's not. On purpose. I'm …

—This is Becky Rasbatch. I've just stepped out. Probably to kill myself. Leave your name and number, and I'll get back to you, if not in this world then the next. Wait for it. (*Bleep*)

—Damn it, Becky. I feel bad enough as it is. Please stop making things worse for both of us. There is no need for all this grief. Every drama has a final curtain. All that matters is that we live to the full the parts we get to play. Then move on to the next role life offers us. Listen, muffin, I really do need my phone free and my tape empty for business calls. That's vital. It's tough being an actor. It's murder. So please be good. Agreed? So that's that, then. Take care.

—This is Claude Shell. I'm out. Tell me who you are, and I'll call you back when I'm in. If it's business, great. But if it's anything more or less otherwise, *don't*. Don't wait for the *bleep*, and don't saying anything after it *comes*. Okay? (*Bleep*)

—Is this the Mr. C. Shell on the seashore who is so suave and dimple chinned in that wonderful vodka fantasy I saw in the commercial break during the late-night horror film on TV? I was thrilled. "See that actor? He was my lovey-dovey until the whole thing crashed recently," I said to my neighbor, Teona, from downstairs, who was also thrilled. "What's he like?" she asked. "Bit frightened, actually. Has one eye on the exit even when in bed. Give him a smile, and he bolts for the door. And boy, can he economize. Eliminates all those farewell-I'm-dumping-you phone calls. Must save him a small fortune." That's what I said to her, Claude. But, darling, do you know I've changed my mind? I don't want you to ring me after all, because it would just be to get my anguished voice the hell out of your stupid tape-recorded life so you can be left in peace to pursue mega fame and fortune to the very ends of the stupid earth. But the thought of contributing a daily, personal newsletter into your very own tape recorder greatly appeals to me. I feel cheered up already. Saved by the bell, you might say. Or do I mean bleep? How wonderful to know that I will be able to tell you all about my sorrows and joys, triumphs and setbacks, knowing you will always be there, my darling, to listen. *Adieu, mon cher,* until tomorrow.

—This is Becky Rasbatch. How are you today? I can't come to the phone right now having been swept up in the great social swirl that is my exciting nightlife. But give me a hint, and I'll give you a ring. When I've regained my strength, that is. I will now hum some Cole Porter until the bleep. Humnnnn, hum, hububumnnnnnnnnnnnnnn … (*Bleep*)

—Get out of my life, you hear me, and leave my goddamn phone alone, understand? I'll call the police. I'll get a court order. I don't want to hear from you ever again. And I don't give a flying fuck about your precious problems. I'm losing work because of you. So butt out. Take off. Scat. Got that? Disappear. Good-bye forever. Okay? This is Claude.

—Anita Shell speaking. As some of you will know, I am Claude's mother. My son, unfortunately, is in the hospital with a severe skin rash. Rather nasty, actually. But the doctors have assured me that the prognosis is excellent, for which, I know, we are all grateful. If you wish to leave a message of sympathy or encouragement, I will endeavor to convey it to Claude in person. Thank you for calling, and please, before you speak, would you wait for the electronic signal that will, I believe, announce itself in the form of a bleep. (*Bleep*)

—Oh, hon. I'm so sorry to hear about you severe skin rash. What rotten luck. How could this have happened? Well, I'm sure it will be just a slight bleep in your climb to the top. I think I mean blip. A slight blip in your climb to the top. When you spoke to me recently of not giving so much as an airborne copulation about my personal concerns, I knew something was amiss. It was so not like you, Claude. No matter. You'll feel much better, I'm sure, when you're back in your own place amid your familiar surroundings. Get well soon, sweetheart. And when you do come home, don't worry; I'll phone you—I promise. So hang in there. Many kisses from a great admirer, your very own true love, Becky Rasbatch.

Coming Attractions

The first day I was taken as a child to our local movie house it became for me nothing less than the Promised Land. Named the Tobart Palace, it stood small and modest on a quiet street in a treeless part of Long Island called Woodside. So small and modest was the cinema that its balcony had just three rows. It was there I learned of the lofty pleasure of sitting above and looking down upon the dark void into which I could see nothing except, at the very front of the orchestra on weekend matinees, those weird kids who sat so close to the screen they looked like silver dwarfs in the quivering light.

The Tobart offered a Saturday children's show, and all my buddies reveled in the fun and fear that awaited them inside. These entertainments contained no sex, nudity, or swearing. No need, for we were under age, after all, and knew all about such things. But I would never again in life be as frightened as I was by those frequent black-and-white horror films. I never wished to go to one, but the management made us an offer we couldn't refuse. Each kid was handed a pledge card with twelve places for punch holes so that if, for eleven Saturday matinees, we went to the Tobart and got our cards punctured eleven times in a row, then, on that last distant Saturday, we got in for free. That was the deal. My dumb, diminutive buddies loved it. Not me. I knew it meant I would have to see every movie on offer for three long summer months, including, of course, those sadistic dramas of unmitigated horror. A weekly series of short episodes involving the Lone Ranger getting surely killed at the end of each and escaping unscathed at the beginning of the next in no way lessened my fear. I knew what was coming, and when it came, I would be scared senseless. In the Promised Land, alas, all is not as we would wish.

In one of these scary movies a group of guests in a stately home had discovered the presence of an unspeakable evil lurking outside in the night. They all gathered in a vast living room to decide what to do. Finally someone with a posh voice and a total absence of problem-solving skills suggested that the best plan was for each of them to return to their rooms, lock their doors, and go to sleep. I nearly shouted, *No, no, stay where you are! There's safety in numbers.* Did they heed my advice? Of course not. And one of them, a lovely blonde with a dress cut as low as her IQ, went to her bedroom where a slowly shifting moonlit tree cast ominous shadows on the French windows. The music grew louder (never a good sign), and there appeared (I knew it, I just knew it) the evil form of a half-human thing that we saw but she didn't. I couldn't watch anymore. With a desperate whisper to the others about needing the john, I sprang from my seat and ran in shame up the narrow aisle of a full house, scurrying to the safety of the empty lobby to cower as unobtrusively as I could until that awful scene was over. I slunk back expecting guffaws of ridicule from my heartless buddies only to find I hadn't been missed. There they all were, motionless like gargoyles in the quivering light. I took my seat like a passenger at the mercy of a reckless pilot, until the music rose, the dread returned, and once again I ran.

After escaping home to a comforting dinner, I then sat on our front stoop to await the arrival of the ice cream truck with its jangle of bells. At last I climbed into my cozy bed, but now the dark became a menacing place with hideous monsters outside my window or inside my closet waiting to burst in on me with ghoulish glee. When at long last I fell asleep, there came the mute, slow-motion terror of bad dreams.

Years later the Promised Land became the magnificent Valencia Theatre on grim Jamaica Avenue with the endless shade of the elevated train offering loud, rude, random clatter. Even then I knew that Valencia was a city somewhere in Europe. Why it was honored by having its name attached to this indoor oasis on such a sad street was anyone's guess. The very sight of the place excited me with its bold marquee hung with wraparound drapery depicting rows of icicles to entice us from the tyrannical heat into the miracle of air conditioning. The moment you stepped into the lobby, you were offered your first of the many escapes from reality Hollywood had to offer: a permanent building-size chunk of arctic air. The next thing you noticed, high on the surrounding walls, were castle parapets and slanted rooftops that were meant to depict that famed city in Spain. Higher still, if you craned your neck, was a pretense of night sky, the roof pierced with silver dots. But if, alas, you were not yet sixteen, the Promised Land was a bitch to enter.

This was because each kid had to ask a complete stranger, "Mister, would you buy my ticket for me?" then hold out his money to the unknown grown-up standing in line. This plea had to be made without the lady seated behind the glass booth noticing and refusing to accept this illegal transaction. Often when I tried my luck, I encountered one brusque refusal after another, yet I always persisted, mindful of the rewards that awaited me inside.

Entering a movie house back then was to be struck blind. A faceless angel with a flashlight would appear and lead you down the aisle to an empty seat from which the view was partly blocked by the head of the person in front. If not, there came just before the film began (it never failed) a despised latecomer, larger than life, to stand rudely, then sit squarely, in front of you. I remember coins spilled from a pocket that rolled away amid derisive laughter, someone in the silence unwrapping a cacophonous candy bar, the faint yet overpowering smell of popcorn, whisperers silenced by a sibilant "Shhhhhh," and always the brute whose elbow laid claim to your armrest.

On the screen appeared the lyrics of "Row, row, row your boat, gently down the stream" while a bouncing ball landed on each word in time with the music as a lady with a brazen voice led the sing-along, though some of us, those who could not lift let alone carry a tune, remained silent. Next, the portentous newsreel told of sad events from around the world followed by a *Tom and Jerry* cartoon whose frantic characters were repeatedly crushed, flattened, or blown to bits but were always resurrected to their nonsensical selves to bring the mayhem to a stuttering "Th-th-th-that's all, folks."

Going to the movies was my greatest pleasure in those days, and so it didn't surprise me when Miss Swainpole, our history teacher at PS 170, mentioned actors and actresses and the films they appeared in to highlight moral lessons from our country's "glorious past." She slightly resembled Katharine Hepburn and had something of Hepburn's scratchy, androgynous voice.

To demonstrate how we should stand firm in our moral beliefs, should others abandon us, Miss Swainpole singled out the bravery of Gary Cooper in *High Noon*. Or to show how a kind man living a good life can affect, for the better, an entire town, she summoned up modest Jimmy Stewart in *It's a Wonderful Life*. Miss Swainpole was in her element teaching us about Hollywood's romantic absolutes and its heroic demonstrations of right and wrong. She beamed when she spoke of how that most splendid of all men, tall, sad Honest Abe, had been reincarnated by the always-earnest Henry Fonda or the deeply wise Raymond Massey.

As she spoke, she was stared at with fixed curiosity. Whether that inert cluster of children who filled the room once a week had even seen these films was a question she never asked. To her, it was a given that such movie classics were as familiar to us as were her quotes from the Declaration of Independence or the Gettysburg Address, and she no more thought to check if this was the case than it occurred to ask if we had beds to sleep in.

Sitting next to me was fourteen-year-old Bruno Brunetti, who looked perpetually puzzled as if having only a semicomprehension of the world around him, his mouth slightly open, his body language suggesting an eagerness to do or say something, anything, if it would just make Miss Swainpole pleased with him, if only he could work out what that might be. He was lean and muscular, good at sports, and the only one of us who, at softball, had slammed a home run clear over the wall into Parsons Boulevard. The very wall he'd once walked along, like a tightrope, high above the street during lunch period until Mr. O'Malley, the gym teacher, yelled at him to come down from there at once. Shy with girls, boisterous with boys, he tried hard in every class and just barely made the grade.

In the last row, slumped in his seat as if he would much rather be somewhere else, was Zubin Silver, the brightest kid in the room who was a bit embarrassed by how often he was called upon to prove it. He wore eyeglasses like a medal of honor, and his shirt collar was often turned up in back for no good reason. He wasn't much liked except by me, whom he mostly ignored.

I would hate to say Bruno was dumb. If pressed I would have to say, okay, he's dumb, but dumb in a rather interesting way. When the legend of Icarus came up in class, it was news to him, and I'm sure to others. Not Zubin. Indifferent to class participation, he never raised his hand yet always knew the answer. In this case I did too, I thought, yet I wasn't sure, for I tended to confuse the tragedies of Icarus with Sisyphus, not to mention that other Greek chained to a rock so hungry birds could peck at his liver for all eternity.

Miss Swainpole, trying and failing to conjure up the answer to her question, finally pointed her long arm at her best pupil. With a sigh, Zubin sat up, cleared his throat, and explained that Icarus wanted for some reason to escape from the island of Crete and so his helpful father, a bit of a handyman, made him a pair of wings that he stuck to his son's back with globs of wax. Icarus was warned, for reasons any dimwit would understand, not to fly too close to the sun. But he was a smart aleck, Zubin said, and disobeyed his dad for the sheer pleasure of it, and sure enough the sun melted the wax, his wings fell off, and he dropped like a stone into the sea.

Our teacher was pleased. "Well done. May I say that our Mr. Silver, although he editorializes a bit, is a pleasure to listen to." She smiled warmly at her best student while the whole class hated him even more.

That day when Bruno and I were walking home together after school, his mind was clearly still on the legend of Icarus. Bruno said he was willing to bet money that this juvenile delinquent who flew too close to the sun at least got himself a great tan while he was up there larking about. I doubted if scholars throughout the centuries had ever thought of that or whether it would have done them any good if they had. But for my part, I was proud of Bruno for coming up with that offbeat view of things—dumb in an interesting way.

"Should have told Swainpole," I said. "She might have got a kick out of it."

"Or kicked me out for saying it." He demolished thin air with a few roundhouse blows. "Pow, pow, pow."

On another occasion, our fervent teacher described *The Divine Comedy* with its many levels inhabited by increasingly virtuous souls as one climbs toward heaven or the reverse as one descends through the circles of hell to the very bottom level to encounter history's three great traitors: Brutus, Cassius, and Judas.

On the way home, Bruno wanted to know if those circles descended like in that "Whatchamacacallit, that weird museum they got?"

"The Guggenheim?" I ventured.

"Yeah," he said. "I wanna roller-skate down, take the elevator up, and do it again."

"You were there?"

"Naw, saw photos."

"I don't think Swainpole would want the Guggenheim turned into a skating rink."

A flurry of blows by way of agreement: "Powpowpow."

The truth was that our oddball teacher was not above piercing some with slivers of sarcasm while ravishing a favorite with excessive praise. She would even castigate the famous of whom she didn't approve: Napoleon's stupid invasion of freezing Russia or Dickens leaving his poor wife for a younger woman after twenty years of sacred marriage. She encouraged class participation. She would laugh when she was pleased, or, if not, her eyes would flashed with Dantesque doom.

She was no longer young. Perhaps even as much as forty years old. No ring on her finger, I noticed. It was hard to imagine what her life was like when the school day ended. And what on earth did she do with herself during those long, school-free summers? Except, of course, go to the movies. We all knew she did that.

One day, I forget on what pretext, Miss Swainpole lectured us to always help others, offering aid to those in need, ever ready to stand up and be counted, heroes or heroines each and every one. As examples, she gave Moses, who led his people out of slavery; Jesus, who died for all mankind; and Joan of Arc, who drove the English out of France, or nearly did, and who was tried as a heretic and burned at the stake. Bruno's mouth hung open wider than ever as Miss Swainpole went on to speak of lesser mortals, those who braved fire or flood, in peace and war, to help their fellow man.

Taking us by surprise, she exclaimed, "Children, see *The Ten Commandments*." Extolling Charlton Heston, she described how he threw open his arms and parted the mighty waters of the Red Sea like cliffs of a canyon to make an escape route for the fleeing Hebrews. And how Moses, at the end of the film, having done so much for his people, pointed out to them from a hilltop what they had so long been searching for, though he was unable to enter it with them, their great goal, far in the distance, the Promised Land. "Oh, see it. See it."

So as we walked home that day, Bruno said, "Would be great, wouldn't it?"

"To see the movie?"

"To help our fellow man."

Had the strain of homework done him in? I studied anew this Italian-American kid whom we all liked for his odd comments and physical daring yet who was so often stumped by life's conundrums and who now wanted be a hero and fight the forces of evil like those others our teacher had talked about.

"How?" I asked.

"How what?"

"Will you help your fellow man?"

"Beats me. Got any ideas?"

"None at all."

"Thought you were Mr. Bright Guy in class."

"Try Zubin Silver."

"Don't like him."

"Why not?"

"He's got all the answers."

"That's my point."

"I wouldn't ask him the right time. Pow, pow, pow."

"Well, if anyone knows the right time, it's Zubin Silver."

"Okay, I'll ask him."

"Really? For ways to help your fellow man?"

"No, for the right time." He punched my shoulder, laughed like a loon, jumped, and pulled a leaf from a low-hanging branch.

To my surprise, a week later, my father suggested we see the new Charlton Heston flick at the Valencia. My mother refused, claiming the air conditioning would be too cold for her. So off we went, my Dad and I, on that memorable Saturday afternoon during a rare May heat wave to Jamaica Avenue with its noise and grime and iron grillwork that imprinted on the street below a constant dappled shade.

We approached the glass ticket window behind which sat that same poor woman with one eye always squinting with suspicion, the other wide open with moral disapproval. Then I heard someone say, "Mister, would you buy my ticket for me?" It was a familiar voice. I turned, and there, in the same plaid shirt he often wore in class, stood Zubin Silver. I hardly knew him but was delighted by this chance encounter. When he saw me, he did what I had never seen him do before: he gave a nod of mild recognition.

"Hey, my dad will buy you your ticket."

"I will, will I?"

"He's my friend."

"Are you his friend?" my father asked, leaning forward with mock suspicion.

"Now more than ever." He held out his money.

"No, no, if you're my son's friend, you're our guest."

I was delighted.

"Thank you, sir," Zubin replied, as cool as in class and not half as grateful as he should have been.

We strolled past the man who tore in half the tickets my father gave him, handing back the stubs.

I said, "So you came to watch mighty Moses part the Red Sea."

"Rumor has it that something more exciting will happen this afternoon."

"You mean he tries and fails?"

Zubin mimicked an old Jew, perhaps his father. "Listen, don't change history; history don't change. It's bad enough as it is."

"If it's nothing to do with the film, I can hardly wait."

"Same here."

In the lobby were photos of film gods: Humphrey Bogart (weatherworn), James Cagney (cocky), Cary Grant (jaunty), Bette Davis (daunting).

By way of repayment, Zubin asked if he could buy us popcorn or something. My father wouldn't hear of it, and, after a huddled conference at the candy counter, he bought Zubin a Baby Ruth and me a box of chocolate-covered raisins.

We chose the balcony, high and steep, and settled in the front row with me between them. The bouncing ball had begun. None of us joined in. The lady sang, the music swelled, the place darkened, and the hectic newsreel was upon us. The raisins were delicious for a time, then less so. Eisenhower sat and signed a bill. There was a flood in Mississippi and a fire in Cairo. We watched a stilted fashion show. The Dodgers beat the Giants 5 to 4. A raucous cartoon finally ended, and the curtain closed for a short time, signaling the film was about to start. The Valencia became more black than night. Dim exit signs increased the ink-dark void. At that very moment, it happened.

A catastrophe of light tore through the wall of the theater like a wrecking ball as a massive chunk of day burst in. This hemorrhage of raw sun, like a convulsive splash of acid, ignited a huge rectangle on the carpet, and we saw, like desperate rodents, a rush of dwarfs, children, ten or more, dashing this way and that, spilling in from the street to find safety in the dark theater while hurrying usherettes descended the aisles trying to catch them.

Only now did we understand that the double exit doors had been opened from the inside, and for a breathtaking moment the brazen world had rushed in. The breach in the wall was slammed shut with a clank of bars, killing the light. It was over. Now an even deeper blindness engulfed the theater. Nervous murmurings of laughter were heard, whispered speculations and a sense of relief.

"Was I right?" Zubin asked, giving a thumbs-up. "The perfect inside job."

"You know who did it?" I asked.

"Bruno, who else?"

"Who?" my father asked, leaning over.

"One of our schoolmates," I said.

"How do you know?"

Zubin turned to him. "He had a plan to get poor kids in free."

"Why didn't he include us?" I asked, a bit peeved.

"'Cause we're not poor."

"I wouldn't go so far as to say that," my father shot back.

"Could have asked us anyway," I persisted.

"Sure, and get you both expelled and tossed in the slammer."

We were roundly hushed. *The Ten Commandments* had begun.

That was Saturday, and I was never so eager for Monday to come. History, the last class of the day, finally arrived, and I was one of the first to enter the room. Bruno had to take a remedial math class across the hall and usually got here ahead of me. His seat was empty. Others ambled in. Zubin Silver made his skulking entrance and, for the first time, gave me a sly smile. We all waited. As the bell rang, Swainpole usually swept in from stage right smiling with enthusiasm. Not today. She entered almost regretfully and gazed at us with a long pause as if not sure who we were.

"Children, we are one less this afternoon. Mr. Bruno Brunetti will not be with us. He has fallen afoul of the law. The police subsequently freed him on his own recognizance after notifying his father. That did not, alas, end this sorry tale. On Sunday, he ran away from home." There was an intake of air. "Now listen please. Should any of you learn of his whereabouts, you must inform the authorities, by whom I mean the school principal, Miss Tenrosen, the police department, or myself. If not, you will become, I'm afraid, an accessory to a crime. Enough said." She took her seat behind the desk, folded her hands on its scarred surface, and stared out the window.

"A calamity," she added, remaining motionless. None of us moved either.

At last she spoke. "There is a heartrending Italian movie by Vittorio De Sica that tells of a poor man who needs his bicycle to make his living. It is stolen from him, and in despair he steals someone else's, gets caught, and is arrested. He is not really a bicycle thief, which is the name of the film, but a desperate man trying to support his son, his wife, and himself. He is as much a victim as the man he stole from. However, there was simply no need for what Mr. Brunetti did. No need. Now," she added, as if a moral obligation had been put aside and forgotten, "who has read and understood the chapter I assigned on Friday entitled 'Manifest Destiny'?"

We heard no more about Bruno. Nor did we see him again. There were rumors, of course. That his father had tried to whip him with a trouser belt but that Bruno had escaped by jumping from their second-story window onto a parked truck. That he'd joined the Coast Guard. That he'd joined the circus.

Eventually we all left and went to high school; some, then, to college. In time I acquired, unaware and with no effort on my part, a kind of maturity. It was achieved with the help of jobs, women, and the wider world. Years later, I returned, as I often did, to visit my parents, who still lived in the same house I grew up in. During one of those visits, on a Saturday afternoon, I went alone for old times' sake to a favorite haunt. Approaching the now somehow less than magnificent Valencia Theater, I pulled out my wallet, stepped up to the ticket booth, and heard, "Mister, would you buy my ticket for me?"

I glanced down, and there I was, my former self, looking up at me, the man he would become someday if he wasn't careful. We went in together, and I handed him his ticket stub. With a mumble of thanks, he strolled off to the candy counter with a loose shoelace snaking after him. He passed new portraits of today's movie stars like so many Greek gods who, as I now knew, were just as badly behaved.

It was a week later at home in my apartment in New York, watching on the living room TV the slowly moving cast list at the end of a hyperactive James Bond film—my two kids arguing, my wife yelling for them to go to bed—when I sat up and pressed the pause button to halt the procession. There it was, shimmering in small white letters on a black background toward the end of the parade of all the participants who had taken part in the making of the movie. Last on that list were the stunt men. The first named, of several, was Bruno Brunetti.

"What is it?" my wife asked.

"Huh?"

"What's the matter?"

"An old friend from long ago."

"Who?"

"There. See? From grammar school."

I started to explain, but she had to leave the room to break up another dispute, leaving me standing now, staring at the set, holding the remote. Then she returned and laughed.

"Hey," she said, "your mouth is open."

A Pre-existing Condition

Robbing banks was popular once, but no one thought to knock off a hospital until Zack Dibble had a try. He put his old man in a wheelchair, pushed him into the lobby of John the Baptist Medical Center, pulled out a Colt .38, and, as in crime films of old, yelled, "Freeze!" No one screamed or fled or fainted. To his immense relief the two startled women behind the check-in desk did just that. They froze.

"I want a heart bypass for my dad," he rasped, "and I want it now."

In the wheelchair, as if none of this had anything to do with him, sat Oscar Dibble, pale as marble. His son lifted from his lap the chest x-rays and the other documents they had acquired from their family GP who had treated Oscar after his heart attack. Days later Zack had tried to get his father into John the Baptist for a bypass. Without health coverage, they had been turned away.

It all had started when Oscar Dibble, to collect the money owed him by his youngest son, Ruben, had climbed the six flights to where the boy lived in an apartment owned by a Puerto Rican woman who worked at the A&P. Together they had been watching a tense episode of *ER* on TV when there had been a knock—more like a punch—on the door. Ruben had opened it and seen his father kneeling, his face against the carpet of the hallway as if peering through a peephole at some riveting spectacle below.

"Dad, what are you doing?"

"Pain."

"Where?"

"Chest."

"What should I do?"

"Pay the sixty bucks you owe me."

The next day, when dye had been injected into Oscar's bloodstream, his doctor, studying a screen that revealed the ghostly tubes connected to the old man's heart, had announced, "Oscar, I kid you not, these are arteries from hell." Action had to be taken, or their father would soon have a myocardial infarction. "What's that?" both brothers had asked. The doctor had sighed. "A heart attack, big time."

There was, as always, no money. Zack worked in a real estate office where the market seemed always sluggish. In all of his twenty years as a driving instructor, Oscar never did have more than several hundred in the bank. Ruben liked to claim he was "self-unemployed." In Zack's words, Ruben looked "as if he had come in third in an Atlantic City Brad Pitt look-alike contest." This resemblance never got him very far except with women. He did odd jobs when the spirit moved him and was not above a little recreational shoplifting. He had a soft spot for children, loved all sports, and never forgot an insult. Once, in Jefferson Park, he had been arrested for accidentally hitting a policeman in the head with a Frisbee. There had been general applause when Ruben had been led away because a number of others had also been hit. Afterward, though not yet twenty-five, he'd drawn up his will with instructions that a bench be placed where the incident had happened displaying a commemorative plaque that read, "This bench is dedicated to Ruben Dibble, who hated this park and everyone in it."

Ruben's wastrel life was something Zack had long since given up trying to change. In many ways he was Ruben's mirror opposite even to the point of having, as his younger brother once pointed out, "all the charisma of a swizzle stick." Of the two, their mother's death hit

Zack the hardest, oppressing him with a phalanx of worries, real and imagined. He was conscientious, hardworking, and reliable, which had earned him his father's respect. Ruben, who drifted through life with a quip and a smile, had won his father's love, a love that only faltered when Ruben owed him money. Among his many other deficiencies, Ruben was rarely on time, and if there had ever been a morning Zack had needed him to be prompt, this was it. Ruben had promised to join them at nine o'clock with a borrowed shotgun. "I'll be there, okay? Relax."

"Ten more minutes, give him," Oscar had pleaded. Zack had done just that. Then he'd drawn his gun and rolled his father at the glass doors of the hospital, which had parted like the Red Sea.

Unlike his brother, Zack had never made a will. Now he regretted not doing so, because once inside the lobby he was gripped by the absolute certainty that this absurd plan would in no way save his father's life. It would simply bring an end to his own. If such was to be his fate, he would kick himself for not making it known he wished to leave his sound system to his old friend William Teel, who loved classical music as much as he did. Zack stood ashen and vacant amid a swirl of silence, the gun heavy in his moist hand, the two women at reception immobile as mannequins.

"I want a bypass for my dad, and I want it now."

This macho demand, prepared in advance and rehearsed at home, became when spoken aloud a bad joke, not even a joke, an embarrassment, painful and pathetic. Nothing happened. No one moved. Finally one of the women lurched into action like an actress belatedly hearing her cue. She stepped from behind the desk (a lovely nurse, Zack noted) and in the lobby's vast silence pleaded for calm. She then instructed her frozen colleague to please page Mr. O'Brien.

Zack stared at the nurse with a rush of gratitude. Her bright, bogus smile was as real to him as the summer sun. In his confusion, she had become his ally. She offered healing and compassion. If this was to be his final day on earth, her shapely presence, her profound kindness, her startling eyes, her selfless courage would be his compensation.

Mr. O'Brien, the nervous hospital manager, must have been nearby, for he appeared within moments of being summoned. Zack repeated his demand. The hospital manager ordered the intruders to leave. Only then did he notice the gun. He was, on the instant, transformed. As if confronted by two visiting dignitaries, he promptly escorted them to the cardiac ward. The nurse pushed Oscar's wheelchair as she followed the purposeful Mr. O'Brien while Zack brought up the rear, dancing and glancing in all directions. The moment the elevator door closed, the receptionist dialed 811 then 901 then 711. Finally, tapping the numbers ever so carefully and this time correctly, she reached the police and screamed.

In the operating theater, Dr. Ramsgate, the head surgeon, tall, bald, and overbearing, was getting ready for his first operation of the day when he and his team were confronted, at gunpoint, with a demand to perform an immediate heart bypass. They were handed x-rays and medical documents. Outraged and blustering, the surgeon announced that this was out of the question. Didn't they realize that without lengthy preparations for such a serious operation, the patient would almost certainly die?

"As will you, Doc, if you don't get started."

"He was always tense, even as a child," Oscar explained. "Please do as he says."

"Are you mad? The police will be here any minute," Dr. Ramsgate warned the gunman, then looked at Mr. O'Brien, who nodded.

"Which is why I'm holding this nurse hostage." Zack's arm went round her waist. "Start now or she dies too. What's your name, Miss?"

"Why?"

"Come on, what's your name?"

"Schubert."

"Like the composer?"

"Yes."

A furious Ramsgate protested, not on her behalf but his own. "Killing me would be a horrible waste," he boomed, as if informing all mankind of the enormity of the loss.

"A most horrible waste," Nurse Schubert agreed, "so to avoid that happening, shouldn't we start?" That settled it, and Ramsgate, who was against waste of any kind, climbed down from his plinth of outrage.

The staff followed his lead and made hurried preparations. Zack was gobsmacked. Was it actually happening? Good God, it was actually happening. To be on the safe side, he insisted he be dressed in a mask and gown like everyone else. This, he reasoned, would make him less identifiable as the gunman when the police burst in. As Oscar was made ready, he thanked his son for getting him this far. "And please, you take care …" Love brimming over, he faltered.

"Don't worry about me, Pop.",

But his father finished with "… of your brother."

"Oh, I'll take care of him all right" was his unflinching reply. "Have no fear of that."

Oddly enough, the idea for this absurd plan had popped out as a joke some weeks ago when they had been bemoaning Oscar's initial rejection by the John the Baptist Medical Center. "We should storm the place," Ruben had cracked, "and make 'em do it for free like in Canada."

"Or England," Zack said.

"Or France," their father added.

"Or all of Australia," Ruben concluded, arms wide.

They enjoyed this bubble of fantasy until Zack punctured the idea as being totally crazy.

"Why?" Ruben shouted. "Better than Pop dying at home. We end up in the slammer, so what? We did it for dear old Dad."

Zack told him to be serious. Gasping for air, Oscar conceded there was no other way to get medical help, yet he did not want his sons going to the slammer. "Let *us* worry about that, Pops," Ruben said, and to push the idea forward, he suggested they use the Colt .38

he'd won at poker on Christmas Eve. They argued for days, yet crazy as it seemed, Ruben's plan appeared to be their father's only hope. And time was running out. Though Oscar had absolutely forbidden them from doing it, the idea had taken on a momentum of its own, and his increasingly labored breathing had sealed the deal. Finally they'd sat at the kitchen table in a grim tableau of mute agreement.

That was how Zack had ended up dressed like an albino terrorist as Dr. Ramsgate perused Oscar's medical history and snapped the stiffly buckling x-rays against a lit screen to peer at his insides. Finally the time had come, and he stood poised above his unconscious patient, scalpel at the ready. At that moment Detective Justin Helmsly yelled, "Freeze!" as he and a rush of men in flak jackets wedged their way into the operating theater.

"Where's the goddamned gunman?" demanded a baffled Helmsly of this renegade gang of masked angels.

Zack clutched Nurse Schubert even tighter and whispered, "Don't worry, I won't hurt you." Then, putting his gun to her head, he yelled through his surgical mask, "Back off, or I'll shoot." He was aware of her soft waist even as their guns swiveled in his direction, promising a loud and imminent doom.

The nervous and usually talkative hospital manager, rendered catatonic since his early-morning trauma, broke the silence with a burst of speech: "Wait, wait. No killing. Absolutely no killing. This is a theater of operation, and this is our most eminent surgeon. Let him do his work. Later you can arrest the entire hospital, for all I care. So like the man says, back off."

Emboldened by praise, Dr. Ramsgate excoriated Detective Helmsly and everyone under his command: "Out. You bring infection in here. Out."

Helmsly had an open mind. But only just. "Yeah? Well, the hell with it. There's no escape, see? When this freakin' farce is over, we will freakin' return. Okay?" Then he and his flock wedged their way out.

Zack rediscovered a pleasing sensation: he was breathing again. Flushed, tingling, and alive, he apologized to his hostage, who was more affronted than frightened.

"I suppose I should thank you for not shooting me."

"I said I wouldn't. I never will."

"Then let go of me."

"Can't. You're my hostage."

"Hold my wrist then. I prefer not to be groped."

"I wasn't …"

"A woman knows when she's being groped."

"Sorry." He gripped her bone-hard wrist. "Look, can I hold your hand instead? Please."

"How'd you ever get the balls to walk in here with a gun?" She took hold of his hand as if to lead a child across the street. So pleased was he by this concession that for a moment he couldn't speak.

The operation would take hours, he was told, and not eager to watch, he took Nurse Schubert with him to check out the intensive care ward where Oscar would be taken next. They walked there hand in hand, and he wished he could take her with him wherever he went for the rest of his life.

"Must you keep holding me?" she asked, removing her mask. "I won't run away." The high-cheekboned beauty of her smooth face stunned him again. She smiled as if she understood him completely and found his urge to possess her so utterly hopeless as to be amusing.

"I must. It gives me strength."

"Oh, well, then, if it gives you strength."

She placed her mask with his in her side pocket as some hospital attendants, at the far end of the hall, watched them cautiously. In the intensive care ward, all the beds but one were empty. An alarming number of tubes and drips were attached to a sallow, sunken, immobile old man who looked as if it took all his strength just to lie there. He opened one eye, then the other.

"You must be the gunman I heard about. Young man, you've achieved a medical breakthrough and not a moment too soon.

Name's Lastfogel, Sid Lastfogel. One favor I ask: if you must shoot a hostage, make it me, not her."

"Why?"

"I've got cancer big time. Pain? You wouldn't believe the pain. What are they doing, these big shot doctors? They're fighting to keep the cancer alive. Why? 'Cause there's nothing left of me to save. They don't give a damn what I think. When I say I want to die, they're offended. They intend to keep me breathing whether I like it or not. This is agony, I say. We gave you pain-killers, they say. Not enough, I say. Well, we can't give you more. More would kill you. See what I'm up against? So make me a hostage. Please. It's my only chance."

"Look, one is all I need. Some other time, maybe."

"Point taken," Lastfogel said. "But when you give yourself up, slip me the gun first, okay?"

"That's assisted suicide. They could jail me for that."

"You crazy? Already you've broken more laws than the Third Reich. You're doing twenty years however you slice it."

A young doctor excused his way in to explain that it was time to monitor Lastfogel's life signs. He glanced nervously at the psychopath standing hand in hand with Nurse Schubert as if they were lovers. When he was done, and before he left, he suggested, ever so delicately, that it was against hospital rules even for relatives to visit intensive care.

"See? They not only want me in constant pain but in solitary confinement. They get their kicks tormenting the sick. Aren't people something? The bad are bad. Okay, I can live with that. But the good are worse. They wield their morals like knives. And get paid big bucks. So what's your name?"

"Zack Dibble."

"Your father gives driving lessons?"

"Yeah."

"Taught my niece. Taught her good too."

This spurred Zack to check on his father. Pulling his hostage with one hand and burdened with the weight of his gun in the other, he left the room. Walking through the hallway, he asked what her first name was. When she said it was Joy, he exclaimed, "Really, that's what I feel when I look at you. May I call you that?" She agreed if in return she could call him Jack.

"Zack," he corrected.

Was she trying to humanize their relationship so he would be less likely to harm her? He hoped so. He was beguiled by this spunky woman whose presence, he believed, would keep him safe, so beguiled that he lost his way and she had to steer him through the right doorway. Dr. Ramsgate was still at work with his circle of assistants, one of whom slapped a pair of scissors into his open palm and then vigorously waved the intruders away.

While passing a window in the hallway, activity in the street caught their attention. There were flashing police cars and yellow ribbons holding back a large crowd.

"All because of you, Zack." She smiled. "Some have fame thrust upon them."

"Some would love to thrust it right back."

"Your dad has no health insurance, right?"

"Bingo."

"Problem is some will see all this as a crime."

"Some would let Pop die. That's the real crime."

"Yes, but this way people might get hurt."

"No one but me will get hurt."

"How can you be so sure?"

"It's the one thing in life I've never doubted."

"How sad. Why?"

"Well, I am an only child, unlike my brother."

"That doesn't make sense."

"Maybe not, but it's true."

"You mean that's how lonely you feel?"

"Exactly."

"How awful."

"Not something you tell people."

"Come with me."

Joy led him to an alcove where, at the push of a button, a machine filled two Styrofoam cups of coffee. Then she led him to an empty room with an eye chart on the wall and a couch in the corner. They sat on its creaking leather and talked. He laid the gun on his left side while she sat on his right. As they talked, his tingling fear lessened somewhat, and he no longer had to breathe deeply to breathe at all. Did she pity him, this hapless loser with his now empty Styrofoam cup? Or had she been won over by what she perceived as his brave recklessness? Was this why his brother did so well with women?

She asked him about his life, and he offered selected snippets to hide the fact that his was the most boring story ever told. In return, she revealed she was twenty-two, born in New Jersey, and, while touching his arm for emphasis (how thrilling), promised to testify in court that he was the bravest man she had ever met, that he had promised not to shoot her, and that he was willing to go to any length to save his father's life, even to laying down his own. She might just be saying this to secure her own safety. But then again, she might not.

An hour had passed, and again he decided to see how Oscar was doing. They discovered that the operation was finished and that his father had been moved to intensive care. They found him lying in a bed next to Lastfogel, who was asleep or dead.

"Hey, Pop. How do you feel?"

"Terrible. Why you holding that girl like that?"

"Don't you remember? She's my hostage."

"Still? It's over, no? You did it, kid. Mazel tov. So play it safe. Give yourself up."

"Your dad's right," Joy said.

"What's the rush?"

"You afraid?" Oscar asked.

"Your son isn't afraid of anything," she insisted.

"Hear from Ruben?" Oscar asked.

"Of course not."

"I'm worried."

"Why? Afraid he fell asleep under his sun lamp?"

"That's unfair."

"You're tellin' me."

A black nurse in glasses appeared in the doorway and called out, "Joy, quick, check out the TV."

She led Zack down the hall to where a huge Sony was broadcasting an event of great excitement to an alcove of empty seats. With controlled fervor, his head shifting with every phrase, a reporter was describing the hospital break-in by a gunman determined to get free treatment for his sick father. The drama had been ongoing for many hours, the situation was tense, and the building was surrounded by the police. The reporter announced that standing next to him was the brother of the gunman, and, sure enough, with a slight widening of the camera angle there stood a smiling Ruben Dibble—in a suit and tie, no less—exuding the pleasure of his own company as he spoke of a deep concern for his brother, who was putting his life at risk to save their sick dad.

"That's my suit he's wearing," Zack said.

Ruben continued with all the sincerity of a politician praising the local hero he had never met. "My brother is a prince, a great American who has never before committed a crime and never will again." He was in his element and, to Zack's surprise, looked even better on TV than he did in real life. That damned camera was as receptive to his charm as young women were. "This country should be grateful to my brother for dramatizing the plight of millions of folks who, through no fault of their own, are seriously ill and unable to afford medical treatment. These are good people who, because of political heartlessness, must die or take action. All Americans should thank Zack Dibble and reward him for his bravery on their behalf, and they should also thank my father, Oscar Dibble, for having the courage to take part in such a desperate plan. If we as Americans don't show our gratitude to these two courageous men for what they have done for us, if we do not pay them back with our heartfelt support, then, to update the immortal words of Winston Churchill, never have so many owed so much to so few and defaulted on payment."

"He's charming," Joy whispered.

"Really?"

"And so committed."

With the applause from people in the street subsiding, the reporter ventured a question, but Ruben ploughed on. "Let me say this. I hereby offer to go in and negotiate my brother's surrender and assure America that Pop is okay."

"Forceful too," Joy added.

Desperate to distract her from his brother's charisma, Zack was about to suggest they return to intensive care when the reporter placed a hand to his earpiece and said, "Wait a minute, word is coming through that a Texan millionaire has offered to pay all the medical bills for what is now being called the Handgun Heart Surgery. Also Senator Harry Reid has just announced he will invite a member of the Dibble family to appear at a subcommittee hearing on health care and that he will try to arrange for a personal meeting with newly elected President Obama." Then the broadcast returned to the studio newsroom where a placid, well-groomed blonde, hypnotized by the teleprompter, told of reports coming in that a copycat holdup in a Mississippi hospital was now in progress. Three gunmen were demanding their uncle be given an immediate kidney transplant. "When we receive further news," she said vacantly, "we will bring it right to you." Next, an aging Republican senator, gray hair aflutter, was making an announcement on the windy Capitol steps requesting that Congress hold an urgent meeting to discuss the Dibble crisis. He feared that a financial solution, as offered by an unnamed California millionaire, would only increase copycat assaults across the nation.

All at once Zack saw the future, and it was scary. Surely they would have to eliminate him to bring a halt to this idea of free medical treatment at the barrel of a gun. Nip it in the bud by killing him right now. To surrender might only expedite his demise. There was no escape.

A hospital orderly stepped through a doorway holding out a cell phone. "Call for you, Mr. Dibble, sir." Zack put it to his ear and heard Detective Helmsley demanding he give himself up right this minute.

"I have a hostage, remember?"

But she was gone. Nowhere in sight. He was alone now more than ever in his whole life. How could she save him if she wasn't here? How, if she was gone, could he ask her to marry him?

"Hostage or no hostage, I'm bringing you in right now."

"I want the press here so you don't shoot me down like a dog."

"Sorry, buddy, time's up."

At the far end of the hall, hunched in helmets and flak jackets, were gunmen creeping in from a door marked EXIT. With the hospital orderly gone as well, Zack placed the phone on the floor and dashed into intensive care.

"This is it, Pop. They're coming to get me."

"So give up, why don't ya?"

"Because they want me dead."

Sid Lastfogel opened his eyes. "What's happening?"

"Where's your cute hostage?" Oscar asked.

"Ran off and left me."

"Women." Sid waved away half of mankind.

"Wait," Zack cried out as the flak jackets entered the room. He pressed his gun against Lastfogel's head. "Back off, or I'll kill 'im."

"Drop it," said Helmsly.

"Kill me," Lastfogel demanded.

"Shush," Zack said.

"Shoot me."

"Shut up."

"Why? It's my life."

"Free that man," Helmsly ordered.

"Shoot, you putz. Somebody shoot me, okay?"

"Hold your fire," the detective ordered.

"Can you believe this? In America they kill each other for sport. But when you're in real need, nothing."

"Please, everybody be calm." This from Nurse Schubert, who had slipped unnoticed into the room. "Dear Zack. Please. It's over. Give me your gun."

There she was, voice soft as fur; bright, magnetic eyes; those concave curves of her cheeks; her beauty bruising his heart as she held out her hand. How could he not give her whatever she wished?

"All right, take it."

"No," Lastfogel yelled, "I *need* it; she doesn't."

"Okay, okay," Zack said, tossing the weapon onto his bed. "But it's—"

"Thank God," Lastfogel cried out, then fumbled, lifted, aimed, and fired at his head with a sharp, mighty, sickening click. It filled the room and paralyzed everyone.

"—not loaded," Zack concluded.

Sitting upright and breathless, tubes hanging from his him like tentacles, he stared at the worthless weight in his trembling hand. "Not loaded?"

"Never was."

"Call a doctor," shouted an orderly in the doorway. "Mr. O'Brien," he said, pointing at the hospital manager out of sight behind him, "has just had a heart attack."

When the trial began, Zack knew he hadn't a hope in hell. Even his lawyer, Ms. Olga Epps, supplied by the Legal Aid Society, a small, thin woman whose thick glasses made her seem to be peering at him from inside an aquarium, even she said he would surely get ten years. That the gun wasn't loaded, that he was selfless in his concern for his father, that Nurse Schubert was willing to testify on his behalf, these hardly mitigated the severity of his crime. The press was mostly against him, stressing the issues of criminal recklessness and the myocardial infarction suffered by the hospital manager. The letters to the editor, however, were largely in Zack's favor. He had been counting on the feisty testimony of Sid Lastfogel. Tragically he had ended his life some months earlier by palming and later swallowing a bottle of pills left on a table while he was being rolled to a different part of the hospital to undergo yet another procedure to keep him alive.

When Zack had surrendered to the police, he had been questioned, booked, and finally given bail. The judge had warned him not to visit the hospital or contact by phone, letter, or e-mail anyone who worked there. Oscar had been released to go home on the same day Zack had gone back to work. The housing market had flatlined, the national economy was staggering, and, he realized, it was only a matter of time before the real estate office he was a vital part of would be forced to close. He visited his father often and occasionally met Ruben there. His brother was in high spirits. He saw himself as a celebrity and was filled with ways to cash in on his popularity with the Democrats and their new health-care legislation as presented by the newly elected president. Facing imprisonment and longing for Joy Schubert, Zack was too depressed to really listen to Ruben or to take an interest in the current banking crisis. All he could think of was living for years in a cramped prison cell with only his useless self for company.

As the prosecuting attorney, a tall, suave Mr. Savage, listed all the counts against the accused—such as illegal possession of a firearm, reckless endangerment, threatening bodily harm, breaking and entering, hostage taking, and causing copycat crimes across the nation—Zack despaired. These were bad enough. Most wounding was the suggestion that his criminal activity had caused such unbearable tension that Mr. J. T. O'Brien, the much-loved and soon-to-retire hospital manager, had suffered a heart attack from which he might never fully recover.

As these crimes were gravely listed, many in the jury box shook their heads as if to say, *What is this world coming to?* As for the defendant demanding a free heart bypass for his father, Mr. Savage lamented the modern-day attitude of entitlement as people increasingly expected something for nothing: free unemployment insurance, free child care, free food stamps, free legal aid, free everything you can think of, including the fabled free lunch. Well, he added, those people were freeloaders who brought shame to the very essence of American freedom.

When Zack's lawyer, the unimpressive Ms. Epps, stood up to present the argument for the defense, she suddenly became a flaming liberal. She did not defend her client as much as accuse the nation of a gross failure in the care of its people. A chill took hold of Zack as Ms. Epps indicted the United States for being sixty years behind all other industrial democracies in establishing a universal health-care system. And, she concluded, if that was "socialism," so was a free education, a free police force, a free fire department, and a free sanitation department. Zack could see that the jury was affronted by such an unfamiliar description of their beloved country. The judge looked as if he yearned to wield his gavel on the head of the nearest socialist. *I am done for,* Zack thought. *It's over.*

Ruben, on the other hand, was now indeed a minor celebrity. He had, to general acclaim, made an appearance in front of a congressional subcommittee where he had spoken movingly of his father as a loyal, God-fearing American, a diligent one-parent provider for his two loving sons, a hardworking driving instructor who now, thank heaven, was slowly regaining his health. Ruben, who rarely had concerned himself with his father, now visited him every day in the hospital, mostly because, on the first of these visits, he had met the enticing Joy Schubert.

On the first day of Zack's trial they were all there, as they were every day afterward. Oscar, looking thin and pale, was seated in the front row with Ms. Schubert beside him in a fetching beige sweater. Ruben was in the back row because, as usual, he had arrived late.

In that heartless courtroom, as the trial continued for another week, it became clear to Zack that the law, he now realized, was not what he had been told it was. In fact, it would knock you down as soon as look at you. It would purr in your ear, then kick you in the groin. It toyed with logic, ignored justice, made a shambles of people's hopes, and was indifferent to their pain. So whenever Joy blew him a few kisses of encouragement, they stung like thorns.

The jury was bussed to John the Baptist Medical Center to visit the crime scene. The prosecution hoped to impress upon them that a modern hospital was civilization's most advanced achievement and that nothing, for whatever reason, should be allowed to interfere with its lofty purpose, which was to be the cutting edge of health care, whatever the cost.

Then, to his surprise, Ms. Epps told him that there had been a serious accident on the Newtown bypass. A pickup truck had collided with the bus carrying the jury back from the hospital and had driven it off the road, where it had rolled over several times. The police had arrested the driver of the truck, a Native American who admitted causing the accident because of a grudge he held against the municipal bus company for denying him health coverage because he only worked part-time. Ms. Epps, eyes swimming with glee deep under the surface of her glasses, was exultant. "What luck. The jury will be dismissed, a new one put in its place, and we start all over again. Don't give up hope."

The trial was postponed for three weeks. Then entering the courtroom, one morning, was the same jury as before. They appeared in casts and slings, and some walked on crutches. They seemed furious at having to be there at all rather than at home recovering from their injuries. Instead they now had to decide on the guilt or innocence of this crackbrained gunman. Zack sensed their anger and felt suicidal.

Early on, he had refused to agree to a plea of temporary insanity or to permit Olga Epps to argue that his father had pressured him into the criminal act for which he now stood accused. All he had wanted was to explain that he'd had no choice other than to do what he'd done. Ms. Epps had warned him that this would be seen as a plea for anarchy, resulting in his certain conviction. So he never had gotten the chance to say in court what he really felt. He was more alone now than he had ever thought possible. How he wished his mother was alive and sitting in the courtroom to warm him with that loving smile of hers, which he remembered mostly from old photographs.

At last the trial ended. Judge Randolph, a frowning and corpulent magistrate who seemed to harbor disgust for all mankind, especially the likes of Zackary Dibble, made a few remarks to the jury that all but pronounced the defendant guilty. He explained that they simply had to decide if the defendant had or had not threatened the staff of the hospital, whether the defendant, by his actions, had or had not endangered the lives of others, including that of his own father. Then the jury was sequestered.

Four hours later they returned stumbling into their seats like a contingent of war veterans. Quick decisions by juries did not bode well for defendants, Ms. Epps remarked offhandedly. She then instructed him to be calm and show no emotion when they pronounced him guilty. As they waited, she kept glancing at her watch as if she had to hurry off to defend other clients as vigorously and unsuccessfully as she had defended him.

"Remember," she said, as an afterthought, "we can always appeal."

Ruben was seated in the front row giving him the old thumbs-up. Joy, in a snug black dress, was beside him wiggling a handful of fingers at Zack, then clasping and shaking her hands in support. But his father, having sprained his ankle, was sadly absent.

Then Olga Epps and Zack Dibble stood up.

"Have you reached a verdict?" the judge snarled at the jury.

A middle-aged woman, her arm in a sling, rose to her feet with a certain withered dignity. "Yes." Her voice cracked and reemerged half an octave higher. "We have."

"Well, what is it?"

"Not guilty, Your Honor."

Gasps, cheers, then powerful applause. The judge was ruddy with outrage. Ruben jumped up and punched the air. Joy clamped both hands over her mouth. Some jurors were smiling. A calm Ms. Epps whispered a suggestion to her client. Empty of all emotion except for a tingling in his face, Zack walked to the jury box. He shook their hands, and some asked him to sign their plaster casts. In the hubbub, things were said that he couldn't hear. One remark he did catch. It came from a juror standing with the help of crutches: "Guess what those bastards at the hospital charged me."

Someone was hugging him; it was Ruben. A kiss on the cheek from Ms. Schubert, a pat on the back from an uncle he'd never liked, many more from strangers, one from the court stenographer, and finally a handshake from a uniformed guard.

"Will you marry me?" he heard himself ask Joy Schubert. It just burst out, so uplifted with bliss was he by her ravishing presence and the dizzying gift of being free again.

Tilting her head to show how deeply moved she was, she said, "Oh, Zack, how can I? I'm engaged to your bother."

Managing to present a travesty of a smile, he finally broke away and took a taxi to his father's place. The sprained ankle, Zack suspected, was something Oscar had concocted so as not to be there to hear the bad news. Indeed, he had no trouble opening the door.

"What happened? What the hell happened?"

"Not guilty," Zack told him.

"They said that? Not guilty?"

"Not guilty."

"Wow."

"Yeah."

They sat at the kitchen table, each with a scotch on the rocks.

"Well, what now?" his father asked.

"Think I'll take a vacation."

"You've got no money."

"I didn't say I'd go anywhere."

"Wait a minute. Yesterday a reporter phoned offering me a small sum to write about our little caper. I bet he'll pay big bucks if you do it. Maybe you *can* go away after all."

"For now, I think I'll just go home."

"Your brother's engaged. To that nurse, remember? Quite a looker. What's her name again?"

"Joy."

"That's right, Joy."

"Plans to live on her salary, does he?"

His father shrugged. "Where else would he live?"

"How's your heart?"

"You always ask that."

"I have no interest in your liver?"

"Would be a change."

"So how is it?"

"My liver?"

"Your heart."

"Better. Not perfect."

"You can hardly sue them."

"Ha. Talk of chutzpah."

"So how are you? Really."

"Okay. Really."

A seismic calamity screamed past in the street.

"More?" He held up the bottle.

"No thanks."

"So you're not guilty."

"That's right."

His father grinned. "Not guilty, but not all that innocent either, eh?"

For the first time in two years Zack Dibble laughed. His head rolled back as if nudged by a memory of carefree youth. It was that secular blessing only humor can give, and in the kitchen, as night came, it did them both a world of good.

CRATERS OF THE MOON MOTEL

Again she directed her husband down the wrong road as she had twice in California and once in Nevada. Tom pulled over, stopped the car, and said she was "an absolutely crap navigator." He had to be in New York on business no later than the sixteenth, so, "Come on, pay attention."

Gail longed to be a competent guide. She had an open map on her knees, but the maddening jigsaw of lines and numbers in this flat paper make-believe of the Northwest in no way related to the erratic road and the lift, dip, and sweep of the real world. There were infrequent road signs, not to mention the impromptu marvels of nature moving past her. And anyway, how important was it that they take this or that turn? Each was heading east, more or less.

"There's a fork coming up," he said. "Do we stay on 26?"

"Stop. We must take a picture of that."

Reluctantly, he did. A dust storm, like an ice-cream cone, was twirling in the distance, beginning to disappear. Lowering the window, she caught it with a slap-click of her Olympus.

She was dressed in a counterculture patchwork of rainbow colors, a heavy necklace of various beads, and earrings of triangular silver shields. He wore the trousers of a summer suit with the jacket hanging from a hook in back. Inside the pocket of his short-sleeved blue shirt was hooked a pen-and-pencil set.

"If we stop every time we see something beautiful, we'll never get home. Do we want the 26 or not?"

The map had fallen into a tent on the floor.

"One moment, Mighty Caesar." After a hunched search: "Yes, we do."

"You sure?"

"I think so."

He examined the map.

"No, we don't. We get off this and turn south. Which way is south, I wonder?" She pointed. "Is it?"

"Yes."

He handed her the map and drove off in wind-buffeting silence, staring ahead fixed and steadfast. A butterfly fluttered up ahead and became a yellow blight on their windshield. Gail sat closer. She blew in his ear. He pretended to be impervious. She made a moronic face of instant rapture. He smiled. She laughed. They quickly, safely kissed. Then he again became fixed and steadfast.

"You look like the young Beethoven."

"I prefer Mighty Caesar."

"Well, beware the Ides of March."

"Send me a memo in February."

"And if I forget?"

"Brutus will remind me."

The road continued to unravel, and, in their air-conditioned bubble, she sensed the heat's intensity by the absence of anything alive on the baked landscape.

An hour later, he frowned at a passing sign. "Lovelock. See where that is."

She took so long to reply he glanced at her. She was staring at him, her hand to her mouth. He stopped and grabbed the map.

"Damn it, we're going north. Do you want me to lose my job? Do you?"

Her reply was a microscopic "No."

He looked at the map again with an exhale of dismay. They would never make the Great Salt Lake by sundown. He remembered something glimpsed a while back. Turning the car around, he raced at top speed and finally had to apply the brakes to keep from passing it.

Craters of the Moon Motel. Vacancy.

Tom climbed out into the brazen heat. The owner was hosing down the parking area. Though six feet tall, he gave the suggestion of a growing boy with his cutoff jeans, short-sleeved shirt, soiled tennis shoes, and no socks. He removed his peaked cap to sleeve-wipe his brow, his blond hair tangled like pasta. Turning off the hose, he let it drop on the hard concrete and came forward.

"Law after you folks?"

"How do you mean?"

"Movin' real fast."

"Wanted to get here while there was still a vacancy. My wife keeps getting us lost."

Gail had joined them. The owner nodded at her.

"Well, you're lucky. There's one room left. Want to see it?"

They followed his ribbed footprints along the dry path and entered one of the cabins. The once off-white, now colorless space had two double beds and, in the bathroom, a cracked mirror.

"We'll take it."

"Where you from?"

"New York."

"Sightseeing?"

"Honeymooning," Tom said.

"That a fact?" Each thumb hooked into an empty belt loop. "Reckon that explains the rush."

Gail smiled.

"How much?"

"Eighty if you use just the one bed."

"Well, if I must, I must." Tom gave his wife a quick wink.

"Should keep her from getting lost for a while."

The melting sun lit a stained-glass sky. Gail stood on the porch of their cabin engrossed in the silent drama. Then, after descending the steps, she unlocked the car's trunk compartment, which bounced open, taking a few ineffectual bites at her like the jaws of a mechanical shark, and retrieved her husband's toiletries' case.

"Did you lock up?" he asked when she returned and held the keys out to him.

"Forgot."

"Gail, there are thieves even out here."

She left the cabin and returned again.

"And the windows too?"

"And the windows too." With that she threw the keys at him. They landed in the shoe on his lap as he worked to untie a tangled knot. He looked up, but she had gone into the bathroom.

He was still there when she came out. Now he was struggling with their crippled Olympus. It had jammed when he'd tried to take a picture of the sunset from their window. *Well, this is one problem he can't blame on me,* she thought, surprised by his grimace and his loose-hanging hair, at how demonical he looked in the light from the table lamp, like a terrorist setting the timer on a car bomb.

As she removed her clothes, she kept glancing at him, but the camera held his attention. She despaired at his ability to ignore her when she could only pretend to ignore him. In bed she continued where she had left off in *Madame Bovary*, using the same lamplight that had struck all gentleness from his face. The noise of a passing car swelled and faded as had her annoyance.

"There," he said. "Done."

She found him smiling and pleased.

"You fixed it," she said. "Wonderful. We'll celebrate, shall we? Let's drink to it."

She tipped the enameled pitcher on the night table until just the briefest splash of water had dropped into his drinking glass. He swirled it, sniffed it, sipped it, paused, and nodded in approval. She poured some into each mug, touched glasses with him and took a discriminating taste herself.

"Subtle. Imported?" he asked.

"Domestic," she said.

The air had cleared, and she was happy. He prepared for bed, humming a song they'd heard in a roadside restaurant where they had stopped for an early dinner. He carefully laid out his clothes until the chair was hidden. In the bathroom he splashed, spit, gargled, roused the toilet, hummed again, and came out wiping his hands on a bath towel.

"We'll keep this for the lake when we swim tomorrow." He rubbed his face in the harsh, blue cloth and threw it into his suitcase.

With a worried laugh she said, "Oh, put it back. I'll want to take another shower tomorrow."

"Use the other one."

Sitting on the foot of the bed in his boxer shorts, he clipped his fingernails.

"Tom, we're not going to keep the towel, are we?"

"Yes, we are."

"It's not right."

"Gail," he said, "it's a towel, not the Turin Shroud. Motels budget for these as nightclubs do for ashtrays. We're being overcharged for this shack anyway."

"It's just, you know, not right."

He stood up. "Like much of life. The president lies and traps us in a stupid war. Our self-righteous governor cavorts with call girls. Executives award themselves big retirement bonuses. You want to change things? Fine. But why start with this? I don't remember you complaining about certain other activities."

"What other activities?"

"We're traveling in a company car. But we're not footing the bill."

"I know," she said, pinching a bit of sheet.

"And that's all right, apparently."

"Well, it's a big company that gives you only three weeks off with pay. But this motel is a tiny business."

"So it's okay to shaft a big company."

"I didn't say it was okay."

"And how about our traveling expenses. The company's being charged for those too. This is supposed to be a business trip."

"I didn't realize that. That doesn't seem right."

"But it's okay to use a company car for pleasure?"

"Well, it's a matter of degree, isn't it?"

"Is it?"

"If we're doing the wrong thing, we should stop. But that doesn't give us the right to take this man's property."

"But he's ripping us off. Can't we at least take a towel at his expense in the same way we take a honeymoon at theirs?" He pointed vaguely toward New York.

"Okay. I think we're wrong on the towel and the car, and we should never have—"

"Oh, please. It was you who turned down your mother's cottage in Vermont. It was you who voted for Paris though we're nearly broke. But then who jumped at the chance, no questions asked, of a free cross-country trip. Would you have given that up?"

She pinched another part of the sheet and said nothing.

"Well?" he asked.

"Yes, I would."

"Really?"

"If you had told me all the facts. Why not?"

"Why not? Because you see morality in simplistic terms."

She found herself staring at the slightly exaggerated indentation in the center of his chest. It seemed unrelated yet linked to the argument: the hollow of fear, an absence of laughter.

"What's wrong with that?" she asked.

"Gives you a piss-poor grip on reality."

"How so?"

"That would take all night."

"Go on," she said acidly. "What else do we have to do?"

"I'm too tired to go into it right now."

"Oh, you're too tired, are you? Well, not half as much as I am."

And she slammed the door behind her after marching into the bathroom.

All night she slept with her back to him, and her first thought on coming awake in the morning was that nothing had changed. Quietly, she dressed in the same clothes she'd worn the day before. Out on the porch, in the already increasing heat, she sat in a torn canvas chair and waited. A Buick and a Volkswagen had joined them in the night. She went to the reception room and fed some coins into a machine. Back in the creaking canvas chair, for the first time in eighteen months, she lit a cigarette. The alarm clock she had borrowed from her mother came alive in the cabin. It was six in the morning, and she felt as lost as a child.

He came out with a touch of shaving cream behind his ear and said good morning too loudly. She said nothing and received a kiss on the cheek. She didn't move. He squatted in front of her, but she stared over his head at the land's desolation.

Looking into the eyes that refused to look at him, he said, "There must be someone home. I see a light in the window."

He performed an assortment of funny faces. No reaction. His face was the map of a foreign land she had been to once but had no wish to return to.

He transported his prisoner in silence, her gaze fixed on a landscape so barren it seemed in a state of bereavement. She, sitting next to him like a dangerous hitchhiker, awakened a fear he had never known before. The warm flow of the morning air rushed past them unabated. She scratched at a stain on her skirt and turned her obdurate face toward the desert again.

His stress grew until at last he brought the car to a halt and trotted across the cracked concrete to enter a wooden dwelling with *STORE* painted in longhand over the entrance. He emerged at once and trotted around to the back. With no need to be there, he stood beside the urinal inside the clapboard shack picking slivers of wood from the unpainted wall. Sure enough, when he returned, she and the car were gone.

He ran and stood on one of the dashes of white in the middle of the road that blended into a single eternal line toward the opposite horizons. The blue Ford was nowhere to be seen. He chewed his nails, walked about, listened. There was only that vacant road and the sound of his breathing. He had forty dollars, a handkerchief, and a comb. In his shirt pocket was the receipt from the motel. He crushed it and threw it away. At last he saw her, the auto appearing before its sound reached him. No, it was a black SUV that sped by with a punishing roar.

He sat on the top rung of a wooden fence, climbing down whenever a car appeared. Within an hour, twelve of them came and abandoned him there. He felt she had taken an essential part of him with her, leaving behind an unprogrammed robot.

The thirteenth car was an old Packard with great semicircular fenders and a high, flat roof. Unlike the others, it stopped and backed up. The driver, in a peaked cap, hunched and straightened his shoulders as he pulled up on the hand brake.

Didn't I pay him? was Tom's hurried thought. *Of course I paid him.*

"Howdy," said the tall man after clearing his throat.

"Yeah," Tom said cautiously.

"Seems you accidentally took one of my towels."

In amazement: "You must be mistaken."

"Nope."

"Perhaps the maid ..."

"The wife does the rooms."

"You can search me if you want."

"Where's your missus at?"

Tom twitched as an MG rocketed by.

"You seem right nervous. Your missus wandered off again?"

"Gone shopping."

"Comin' back at all?"

"Of course she's coming back."

"Hope she ain't lost. Bad luck losin' your bride on your honeymoon and your car in the bargain. Leastways the car's insured."

"I said she's coming back."

"I hear ya."

The heat was rising, and the man loosened his cap and pulled it snug again. "Well, I'll just wait around some."

"We don't have your towel; I told you."

"Be over by the tree."

"You took a long trip for nothing."

"Was on my way to pick up some three-inch nails when I saw you there all by your lonesome." He walked off. Tom followed until they were both in the shade,

"You didn't see a light-blue Ford, did you?"

"Nope. Wouldn't have seen you 'cept you was smack on that fence like a cow on a roof." He leaned against the tree. "You don't know where she's at, do ya?"

"Told you, she's shopping."

"Buyin' you a little surprise, is she?"

"Any minute now she'll be back."

"That a fact? Well, I'm waitin'."

Tom wandered into the bright heat to inspect the long, empty road. He stood there without a wife or a car or the slightest idea what to do next. The old lady who ran the store came out to spill a pail's worth of purple slush into a black ditch. She looked up at him, paused, then the screen door bounced shut again twice.

"Look," Tom said, moving toward the tree. "Since you're obsessed with this crazy idea, the least I can do is reimburse you for your time and trouble. It's a small price to pay to be left in peace. What's the damage?"

"Want my towel is all." He looked offended.

"You can't be serious. Here's ten; take it."

"Towel's part of a set. They all the same."

Wearing a new shirt, the tennis shoes still without socks. "I do not believe this. You just want that one stupid towel back?"

The motel owner said nothing.

"Is that it?"

The man nodded as if ashamed.

"Good God." Tom walked away. He stood by the fence and shouted at the tree. "Well, we haven't got it anyway." There was no reply.

He climbed up and sat down. Four cars later he climbed off the fence to escape the sun and walked back into the cool decay of the outhouse, closing the door behind him. When he returned, the Ford had pulled onto the gravel by the tree and Gail was climbing out. "Oh, there you are," she said to the motel owner. "I gave it to your wife. I'm sorry we took it."

He touched the peak of his cap. "Thank you, ma'am. I see you found your way back here pretty good."

"We're very sorry," she insisted.

He tilted his head. "*Him*, I'm not so sure." Each thumb in an empty belt loop. "It's just that people don't care what's right nowadays."

"I know."

He touched his cap again, and in a moment the Packard was gone. Tom waited for her to look at him. "I wonder if they sell Cokes," she said, glancing at the store.

He bought two bottles, his hands pleasantly cold as he carried them. The sun had taken hold of the land as he pushed his way through the thick heat. She was sitting behind the wheel. She accepted one of the bottles and lifted it to her mouth.

"I'll drive," he said softly.

"I'm here now."

He was seriously ill at ease when not at the wheel, but he didn't argue. Walking to the passenger side, he tapped the door handle with his fingertips. Yesterday afternoon it had been too hot to touch, and he'd had to use his handkerchief to grasp hold. Once inside, he lifted the voluminous map from the floor. As she drove, he stared ahead in silence. Then he directed his attention to plotting the shortest route to the Great Salt Lake.

THE BOOK COLLECTOR

"Please do something," my mother said, her cheerfulness gone, her voice ragged. "Talk to him. I can't live like this."

I knew at once what she meant, for she had lived like this with my father for as long as I could remember. It was a constant that always seemed to grow worse. First in their house on Long Island, which they'd owned, and now in their apartment in Manhattan, which my father had started renting after his heart attack. You entered their apartment and discovered letters, bank statements, newspapers, and magazines occupying almost all the chairs and the entire couch. The latest arrivals went directly to the dining table where usually at one end a bit of space was left for them to cluster round for dinner like refugees.

But this was as nothing compared to the books. Books were everywhere, yet if you wanted one, you couldn't get to it. In front of many books, there were other books piled on their sides in awesome columns, walling in, as it were, the shelved books, which now forever out of sight slowly faded from living memory. It was near impossible to sample any of the volumes from these towering structures unless they were near the top. Trying to pull out one of the others made the columns come alive and sway with the real promise of an avalanche.

Upon entering my father's den one arrived at the very epicenter of chaos. In full view was an expensive hi-fi set that couldn't be reached and an impressive stack of stereo records, lying on their sides, that couldn't be sampled, even if the stereo could be reached, because on top, also on their sides, was a tonnage of art books plus the sketches of Audubon and a boxed two-volume tome detailing, with diagrams, Tutankhamun's tomb. The reason the bookcases and the hi-fi set couldn't be reached was because piles of yet more magazines, thick files, and loose papers presented, if you tried to stand on them, an ever-moving mass.

There had once been a desk in the den. When last seen, it had been entombed with clutter and could not be used as a desk and so was lost to us in much the same way a damaged nuclear reactor was lost when it was sealed up for centuries so no harm could come to those who lived close by. Because a work surface of some sort was absolutely necessary, particularly at peak intake seasons when even the dining room table was piled high, forcing us to eat wherever we could as if at a crowded party, clearly something had to be done. So a card table had been placed in what little space was left in his den, so he could sit and write a check or open mail or … I almost said read. But he never did. Not books. Chaos is a great time consumer, keeping one busy the better part of a lifetime. And at night, with whatever time was left, there was always TV. No, he never read books. Not anymore.

In the beginning he loved them. For what was inside them. The earliest editions in my father's library revealed pencil marks beside ravishing moments in Swinburne or droll arguments of Chesterton or folksy reflections by Montaigne. He bought the first of these volumes with his own money, which he had precious little of, from shabby secondhand bookstores in the subcellar of the Depression. Later he acquired them for free when he became the chief copywriter with an ad agency that specialized in selling books.

"You've got to do something," my mother moaned once again. I said yes, I would, not telling her, of course, that I had already tried some years ago in their house in Queens. The conversation, on that occasion, went like this:

"We have too many books in here, Dad."

"What?" He wasn't deaf, but he often didn't hear me.

"Far too many books."

"Why? What do you mean? I need them."

"You never read them."

"I read them all the time."

"I don't see you reading them."

"You're not always here."

"Ma says you don't read them."

"She's not always here."

"Where is she?"

"She goes out a lot. Shops. She's a very busy person."

I spoke darkly of the accumulation of allergy-creating dust from his library and the ever-increasing weight they placed on the structure of the house. With that I finally reached him, or reached his anxiety, which was the same thing. He said nothing at such moments, changing the topic or wandering away. Two hours later he, with great purpose, came back, a slim, small, frail, fern-colored volume in his hand.

"Do you think we can get rid of this?" he asked.

The title said *Abnormal Psychology.*

"Yes, we can get rid of that."

"Okay," he concluded, as if his job here was done and now he must ride off to other private libraries and help them lessen their bulk. The slim volume was left on the dining room table. The next time I saw it, a year later, it was on one of the living room shelves next to *The Mystery of Mysticism.*

He simply could not throw anything away. He was far too anxious ever to do that. Sometimes I had to remind myself that he didn't invent anxiety. He only perfected it, made it into a way of life that effectively diminished the quality of life. Yet in the real world, which was everywhere outside our home, he flourished. Still, people who flourish because they are driven by demons tend somewhat to overflourish, becoming increasingly successful and increasingly grotesque.

"When?" my mother asked.

"When?"

"Will you talk to him?" But she pressed on, too anxious herself to wait for an answer, repeating how impossible it all was. Dust everywhere. Junk everywhere. Couldn't have guests in. Nothing could be thrown out. There was hardly even space for her things. "Speak to him."

I said I would.

"I don't understand," she exclaimed. "There's no room anymore to do anything."

"Yes, I know."

"Have you looked into his closet?" she asked.

I had, from afar. In his den there was a walk-in, almost a live-in, closet that could well have had above the door the warning "Abandon hope, all ye who try to enter here." The way was blocked by gadget bags and tripods, cameras and strobe lights, several old radios, and a tool chest with boxes of nails, screws, nuts, and bolts. On the shelves were yet more books, and in the rear was a large black file cabinet, locked, its key lost. There was also a damaged zither, an extra hat rack, some unhung pictures, and boxes of what proved to be black-and-white film dating back several decades.

"The humidifier is in there," she lamented.

"And my Staunton chess set. And all my college stuff."

"No, they're in the house in Queens."

"They should be, but they're not."

"Yes, in the trunk upstairs."

"That trunk is in the garage, and it's filled with *National Geographics*."

"Is it? When was that put there?"

"Ma, I was too young to remember."

"*National Geographics?* I thought they were in the record cabinet."

"The *Encyclopedia Britannica* is in the record cabinet."

"Oh, oh, oh," she repeated, quickly, as if three small bubbles of revelation had popped pleasurably in her brain.

Whenever we spoke of their house in Queens, I saw again that narrow, cheerless, semiattached, junk-filled, dusk-lit, book-littered, brick-ugly dwelling with a fenced-in back yard four times the size of a freight elevator.

As I grew, everything around me grew, and in the end I moved out of that brick-ugly house because, among other reasons, there was really no longer room for me. When I took that apartment in the Village, it seemed Japanese in its ostentatious emptiness.

"Talk to him," she requested once more, but what I couldn't say straight out was that, in my opinion, the real cause of her distress was something other than his books or the clutter or her inability to clean. The real trouble, when you came right down to it, was him.

This said, it should also be pointed out that my father had always with him the catastrophe of his own childhood: the escape from a pogrom in Odessa, the arrival in New York not knowing a word of English, and a hysteric as a mother. It had been a protracted assault, and what had emerged, for all to see, was a terrible fear of deprivation. It went were he went like lumbago.

He didn't change his ways, however. Not only did he collect junk, but he also seemed determined to accumulate weight. His bulk mounted steadily, a fact he denied, preferring to accuse the dry cleaners of shrinking his suits. He clung to this argument until good old Sol, whom he hadn't seen in quite a while, dropped in as always without warning, eyed my father, and, with his usual delicacy, cried out, "Jacob, my God you're fat!"

When my uncle left, my father asked, "I'm not fat, am I?"

"Dad, how often have I told you that?"

"You're gross," said my mother.

He sulked and at dinner had two slices of angel food cake.

Soon after that, I flew to Venice with an egocentric journalist to illustrate his travel piece. Poor weather some of the time and his clichéd photo suggestions the rest of the time put me in not the best of moods when I received a knock on the door one morning to be told there was a phone call for me. This, I feared, was a last-minute demand for some further shooting that had not been scheduled when, down at the reception desk, came a long-distance growl from Uncle Sol.

"Are you sitting down?"

There was not a seat in sight.

"Yes," I said, my pulse throbbing. "What happened?"

"Jacob's had a heart attack."

"Is he …?"

"He's doing fine."

"Which hospital?"

"Mount Sinai."

"And my mother?"

"As always."

"So Dad's all right, then."

Sourly: "He's himself again. What can I tell ya?"

"How'd it happen?"

"Couldn't find his checkbook. Had a conniption big time. House is a mess; you could lose a Volkswagen in there. Anyway he felt this blowtorch at his chest. Beryl made him lie down until the ambulance came. Why the hell don't you get him to tidy up the place?"

"I seem to recall trying once or twice."

"And to stop eating like a pig."

"Good idea. Listen, why don't you bring it up next time you speak to him?"

"You're his son."

"You're his brother. Tell them I'm flying home."

"I'll tell 'em."

When I returned, he was sitting up in his hospital bed looking somewhat distracted as if his brush with death had evoked a disturbing image he was now having trouble remembering. For some reason we shook hands, which I can't recall us ever doing before.

"Sorry to bring you back," he said.

"I was on my way home anyway."

"They want me to lose weight," he said, as if asking for a second opinion.

"I'm not surprised. Will you do it?"

"Of course. It's important."

"Well, at least you take their word for it, if not mine."

"What are you talking about? If something important is explained to me properly, I understand."

"So you're going on a diet?"

"I'm already on a diet. They feed you slops here."

The doctors also advised him to move to Manhattan so he could walk to his office and then home again each day. This was done. That is, they acquired and furnished a lovely three-room apartment overlooking the Hudson. But he never did walk to work. In the morning there was not enough time, and in the evening there were too many books to carry.

This was how it came to pass that my parents owned two dwellings in the same city, the larger standing unused most of the year. Their "country home" was convenient enough, God knows, for they didn't have to go into the country to get to it. I often suggested they sell that house, but they hung on to it for safety's sake. If the stock market crashed again and 1929 returned, they could always move back in. After all, the mortgage was paid off. In hard times, what could be safer? I tried to explain that as they grew older they would be less able to travel out to see if their "country home" was still there. But growing older was not part of their plan for the future. The truth was Jacob really didn't care for the house that much, only for the things inside, though he never made use of them. Still, they were his things and, for a reason only he could fathom, were never, ever, to be parted with. This meant my mother now had two dwellings she couldn't clean because of the clutter. And keeping things spotless and in their proper place meant more to her than anything. In the past she had done a thorough clean three times a week with a diligence, almost a desperation, of one who could never quite reach some soiled place, perhaps within herself.

At last it all became too much for her. Those coughing attacks of stifled rage, her endless pleas for reason, her headaches and fatigue, her sense of herself as a failed hausfrau, her despair; all this, I'm sure, led to her illness. It began with a lump behind the ear that grew into a half grapefruit. The growth was removed from her neck in a three-hour operation. The result was a slight left-sided face-slide as if an invisible force were pulling at her cheek and her eye, which she could no longer hold open. My father was marvelous. He was there every day, standing beside her bed for as long as visiting hours allowed and, after he left, winning high praise from the other women in the ward who were puzzled at my mother's less than grateful response to his devotion. In about seven weeks she was finally back where she had been when it all had started, that is, ensconced in the very apartment whose massive clutter had made her sick in the first place.

"Talk to him," she said.

But how? He had walled himself into a fortress of acquisition, which I had placed under siege on several occasions, firing my arguments like arrows, only to grow weary, give up, and go home. So I said to him, rather cautiously, "You know, I think all these books piled everywhere is what caused Mom's cancer."

"What? You're crazy. It was diet. Bad diet causes cancer, or too much sun, or smoking."

"Mom doesn't smoke."

"And she doesn't sun herself either so that leaves diet. Diet causes cancer. Everyone knows that. Diet is everything."

I kept on for a while, then grew weary, gave up, and went home. How on earth was I to proceed? I waited. What for, I didn't know. I achieved, without effort, an almost Zen-like emptiness of mind. Then what I had been waiting for came. It was announced that my parents' building was turning co-op. They could choose to continue living there, paying rent as before, or they could buy. But as renters the apartment could be sold even as they lived in it, sold to someone who must wait, before moving in, until my parents were no more.

"This I don't like," he said. "Our landlord will be someone we won't know, might never meet, and who could choose not to fix things that break. If I fix them, I'll be repairing his place, not mine, and fixing it for free. And what is he doing in the meantime? Waiting around for me to die."

Now, at last, I saw a way to breach the fortress wall.

"Dad, I have the answer. Sell the house and use the money to buy this place."

"Now that," my mother piped up, "is a good idea."

My father said nothing. He was trapped. His fear of having his apartment sold to a stranger with him still in it was balanced by his terrible fear of deprivation, for to put the house on the market he would have to sell, give away, or throw out everything stashed away in each and every room. My mother, who never helped in these matters, even when I was trying to do something for her benefit, wanted to know how selling the house would improve the clutter in their apartment. "One thing at a time," I replied. Later, when we were alone, I said, "My hope is he'll loosen up after letting go of everything in Queens so that the thought of getting rid of just some of his stuff in Manhattan won't be that difficult."

I now worked tirelessly to evoke that mythical absentee landlord who would hover like an uncaring god over my father's very existence.

"How will we get rid of all those books?" he flailed, now semiwilling to consider alternatives.

"Any secondhand book dealer will cart them off in a truck."

"The furniture?"

"In a furniture truck."

"How do we sell the house?" He frowned, as if the process was a new concept in real estate.

"We list it with real estate agents. We hand over the key, and they do the work."

"I will not give a key to a stranger. That's looking for trouble."

"Of course," my mother pronounced with a wise nod as if considering an abstract philosophical problem.

"Whose side are you on? Look, Dad, I'll drive out there to let them in whenever the agent has a prospective customer. I'll be there to see that everything is safe, okay?"

He replied a day and a half later, "Maybe."

There were, I knew, Everests yet to climb, but this was the breakthrough. The next day I drove him out to Queens to inspect the house I hadn't seen in years. It was filled with silent, soulful mustiness. Childhood memories stared at me like ancient tragedies suffered by others. As I examined room after room of clutter, I arrived at the second floor and my father's den. I pushed, the door finally gave way, and there before me was a lifetime supply of God knows what. Cardboard boxes filled the room so that we couldn't even begin to enter. We had been walled out.

"What's all this?" I asked him.

"Books from my office. I had them shipped to Queens."

Evacuating Dunkirk would, in comparison, have been a lightweight exercise in simple logistics. As we left the house several hours later, a man in a shirt as noisy as a rock group stepped out of the adjoining house and called, "Yoo-hoo!" He was a new neighbor who had moved in three years ago, and my father was now laying eyes on him for the very first time. "I vundered, possibly, ven I never saw you, I should maybe write a letter, but I never did, because I hate writing letters. Ah, but there's no need now, is there, 'cause ve meet at last. At last ve meet. Hello."

As we chattered, I longed to get away, my mind bristling with house-selling difficulties, when our newfound neighbor got to the point. "Vud you, perhaps, be considering, ever, to possibly, you know, sell your lovely house?"

"Oh, I'm afraid not," my father replied in his self-satisfied social manner, conveniently forgetting why we were there in the first place.

"We are extremely interested in selling this house," I burst in. "Don't listen to him."

"It is, then, your house, this house?"

"No, it's not my house; it's his house," I said. "He just forgot for a moment what he wants to do with it. He wants to sell it, believe me." And I stared significantly into the neighbor's eye hoping to suggest that my old man was a bit odd but in a lovable way, of course, and shouldn't be judged too harshly.

"Oh, that's right, we might want to sell it, yes," came his somewhat begrudging agreement.

"Right," I almost shouted. "So would you like to come for a drink and perhaps see the place, Mister … Mister …?"

"Farkas," he said with a fine spray, and off we went. Needless to add I was reeling from the serendipity of it all.

My father opened some wine as I showed our guest around. He liked what he saw until he got to the upstairs den where I felt obliged to explain the barrier of books that blocked our way.

Farkas was puzzled. "He took all this here from Manhattan to Queens? Vhat vill he do ven he gets rid of the house?"

"Oh, sell them. My father works in mysterious ways."

"That's okay for God. He's entitled. For the rest of us, it can cost big bucks."

I found myself explaining some of the reasons that made him what he was. The escape from the pogrom to the States, not knowing the language, and getting thrown into the immigrant meat grinder with a mother whose only talent was reaching for and attaining new heights of hysteria.

Sadly he shook his head, as if he knew such tales all too well.

There followed three months of seesaw negotiations during which I was, for my mother's sake, the family adviser, therapist, linesman, and cheerleader. My father swung between paranoid intransigence and resentful though discernible action. Still, the great day was coming, and this made her beam as I had seen her do just once in an old photograph where, at sixteen, holding a half-eaten apple on a New Jersey rooftop, she was delighted by the warmth of a sunlit summer and the promise of tomorrow that could be seen in the distance in the form of the Manhattan skyline.

Finally all the arrangements were made, and the laws delayed us no longer. We went out to Queens to meet Mr. Farkas, sip some of his sweet wine, and sign the papers, an event second in importance in my mind only to the battleship ceremony that ended World War II. Now my father had just eight weeks left to empty the house. I helped as much as I could. The furniture was carted off. The rugs and the kitchen equipment were left in place, purchased by the new owner. A secondhand book dealer came and made an offer that was, as I gave a sigh of relief, accepted. I took my parents to dinner. The battle was won.

The next week I had to go to LA to shoot a story about a film team shooting a drama on surfing. I had never made the trip by car before, so I drove across the country taking eight days to reach the Pacific.

When I returned to New York, I phoned to say I was back. My father was in a state about something, and I realized it had been a while since I'd heard the latest in his constant running battle with his secretary whom he'd continued to employ even in his retirement. But I didn't have the time at the moment to listen to yet another chunk of the saga.

"She's left me," he began.

"Well, get another."

He seemed shocked. "Get another? His own mother leaves me, and he says get another."

"Mom left you?" The hubbub of the world ceased. Life sharpened into focus. "She left you?"

"Come over," he said grimly, "and I'll tell you what happened."

When I walked in, he didn't have to say a word. I saw boxes everywhere, just as there had been in his den when I'd tried to show it to Mr. Farkas. The living room was unusable. The dining table had to be reached via the kitchen. One had to move down the hall sideways. There was even a pyramid of boxes in the bathtub.

"I just kept a few for sentimental value and some first editions," he explained. Then he added, having had a sudden inspiration, "For example, I had to keep your books on photography, didn't I? You don't want me to give those away, do you?"

"What did she say? Or need I ask?"

He gave me a look of painful disbelief. "After forty-seven years, she walks out. Just like that."

"Where'd she go?"

"Is that fair? Is that right?"

"Where did she go?"

"To Selma's, where else?" As always, when referring to his sister in Brooklyn, he waved her away even as he mentioned her name. "You can never trust Selma."

"Do you expect Mom to live in this … this warehouse?"

"Give me a minute, will ya? You're always rushing me. I have to get rid of some old books to make way for these new ones. Don't worry; I'll clear it all up."

"It took you thirty years to get rid of one slim volume on abnormal psychology," I yelled, "and all you did was move it from one room to another."

"What are you talkin' about? I got rid of it."

"You didn't. I can show it to you right now."

"That's a duplicate."

"Oh, for God's sake. Look, will you call Mother? Talk to her."

"You know I can't stand Selma. She wants to know all your business."

"Dad, she knows all your business."

"What if I call and your mother refuses to talk to me? She's a stubborn woman."

"She'll talk to you. And tell her you'll compromise. You'll work things out."

"What if Selma answers? Or that no-good husband of hers?"

"Then give the phone to me."

He was so upset that each time he dialed he had to start again. Finally I took over, then gave the phone back to him without saying a word after Selma had answered and given the phone to my mother without saying a word.

"Where's the Brillo?" my father asked. "I can't find it anywhere … No, I looked under the sink … All right, all right, so I'll buy some more."

I wrote COMPROMISE on the back of an old Brentano's bookmark and showed it to him.

"Listen," he said, "about the boxes. We'll come to a compromise, okay? So just be patient. I'll clear it all up, eventually. What I'm saying is, you don't have to do this. I mean it's okay to come home … Yes, yes, I know about the closets. I'm weeding things out … What do you mean, I'm not weeding things out? I am weeding things out. So, er, when are you coming home?"

My father turned away and, still holding the phone, lifted both hands and dropped them again. "She said she didn't believe me and hung up. Oh, God, that woman is so stubborn."

I suggested we needed a drink and led him sideways down the hall and through the maze of boxes to the kitchen. I uncorked some Chardonnay and put it on the dining room table. I was hunting for two glasses when, displaying his exasperation, he thumped the table with the bottle and sprayed wine all over his jacket. "Damn it. Now look what you've made me do." But when I returned with a tea towel, I saw he was crying.

In time, I was able to get him to sit and sip and listen. I proposed he put all the boxes in storage, then take one box at a time out of storage, empty it of books he wished to keep, fill it with outgoing books, sell that box to the Strand Bookstore, and then take another box of books out of storage and do the same thing. He said this was expensive. I said he had just sold his house and had plenty of money and, anyway, the expense would spur him on. He said a storage house wouldn't let him do that. I said they would certainly let him do that. He said storage houses wouldn't take good care of his books. I said storage houses would take very good care of his books. Storage houses, I said, took poor care of expensive furniture and precious porcelain by hiring people to come in at night to scratch the furniture with bottle tops and crack the porcelain with small wooden mallets, but no one, not warehouse people or skulduggery types of any sort, gave a flying copulation about books, certainly not enough to steal or damage them. I said that only bad governments burned books and even Senator McCarthy wouldn't have gone so far as to do that to our collection of James Branch Cabell, James Fenimore Cooper, Conrad, Lawrence, and Dickens. His entrenched expression was all he had left by way of argument.

"Shall I phone a storage house now?" I asked.

"How will we find one?" was his last feeble attempt at a road block.

"In the yellow pages under storage houses."

"All right, go ahead, but hurry."

When, a few days later, I led my mother back into the apartment, which admittedly looked as cluttered as it had when she'd first phoned to say she couldn't live like this, I do believe it appeared somewhat spacious to her now that all the newly arrived boxes had been removed.

"Isn't it nice?" I asked.

Without comment she vacuumed the carpet. Then she sat down with a cup of coffee. Trying to cheer her up, I said, "You know, with all my recent top-level experience at negotiation perhaps I should try my hand at missile reduction or maybe the Palestine issue."

"You look tired," she told me. "You should rest."

"I'm fine, Ma, just fine."

The next day I had the flu. As I lay in bed with a fever, my father, in an expansive mood, insisted on taking a taxi across town to the Princeton Club to bring me their special hot soup.

"The important thing is one's health," he said, in his attentive bedside manner of lighthearted concern. "Remember—diet is everything."

The Ice Child

"It's marvelous here," she said.

"I knew you'd like it."

"So tranquil. What's it called?"

"In my opinion," he said, "it's pronounced Thaymees."

"Is there a dispute?"

"Let's just say others disagree." He pulled a reed from the ground.

"Others meaning my husband."

"Others as well as your husband."

"How do they pronounce it?"

"Tems," he said. "The River Tems."

"Well, Thaymees does sounds more exotic." She tossed a blade of grass and watched it float away. "Look, you can see the bottom."

"And you can drink the water."

"Where does it come from?"

"From out of the ground, somewhere north."

"And it goes …?"

"To the sea, like all rivers."

"Oh, and feel that," she cried. "I can't get used to it."

"Yes, the wind."

"It's as if the air is making love to me."

"Hold on. That's my job."

"At the moment you seem to be unemployed."

"I mostly work nights, remember?"

"There are places on this planet where the nights are six months long."

"Getting a bit frisky, are you?"

"Perhaps real fresh air is a stimulant."

She smiled as they watched the river sliding past them toward a knob of hills. The trees were suddenly brought alive by a chuff of wind that also corrugated the water and made it twitch with sunlight. She pointed with joy at several fidgety butterflies. Then a few flat-bottomed clouds came by like shipments of eternal peace.

"Oh, did you see what happened?"

"What?"

"That shadow made everything cool. Reading about these things is just not the same. And those wonderful smells and how quiet it all is." She laughed. "Of course, having zero population helps."

"See what I mean? A fortune can be made here. It's beautiful, peaceful, and unclaimed."

"We'll bring them in droves. They'll love it. How could they not?"

"Luckily for us you have the deciding vote," he said.

"Which means you'll become the secretary of land distribution."

"And you, tourist administrator."

She touched his cheek. "Well, thank you, my darling, for showing me all those wonderful places. Let's see, we began at the Big Canyon."

"The Grand Canyon."

"Then we visited ..." She paused to think. "The Ni ... agara Falls."

"Excellent. After that we visited the ..."

"Sara desert."

"Sahara Desert."

"Next we had lunch on that tiny island in the middle of the Passeyfick."

"Pacific. On that point ..."

"You and my husband agree."

She smiled and then recited the other places they had been to. The Great Wall of China. The pyramids in Mexico. And, the most memorable of them all, the excavation site on the island of Manhattan with all those collapsed towers.

"What a tourist attraction they will make," she added softly, almost in awe. "An archaeological find second to none."

The other cities were mostly overgrown mounds just as he had said. But there was still so much to see, and they would be the first to place claims on the best sites.

"A bit of thanks might be in order," he suggested.

"Don't think I'm not grateful to you, to my, let me see, to my loving gust of wind."

"Oh, you can do better than that."

"I'll try again. To my loving windbag."

"Now you've done it. And here I was about to take you to the best place of all."

"Better take me, if you still want my vote."

"Hmmmm. Good point."

He helped her to her feet, and they headed back through the clearing to where the module stood. They climbed in and sat on a couch where he gave the computer its instructions. The downdraft flattened the grass, and soon the Thames, which they followed, became a thread of sliver and the land a patchwork of colors. They came to a huge channel of water, crossed it, and saw land again. They were gaining speed. By the time she dictated a few paragraphs of the Thames River land claim into the machine, he called out, "We're almost there."

They had come to a stark mountain range, a place of austere beauty, with vast canyons of bleached rock majestically indifferent to their perishable selves. They crested several peaks that looked like crude weapons of war, then swung down again through a narrow crevasse that held in its grip a motionless flow of ice.

She, unusually, went quiet. Then he pointed to their destination. She could hardly miss it. It stood in the distance and diminished everything else. They scaled a rock face, frozen and ragged and just yards from their window, until they reached the very top of this majestic presence to settle gently on its white towering peak. The view was vast, harsh, and as fixed as death.

"Welcome to Mount Everest, the tallest on the planet." All she could think of was that this, alone, could make them millions. "Would you believe they put themselves at risk climbing this thing? Some without oxygen."

"Whatever for?" she asked.

"A religious ritual of some sort."

"I thought that man pinned to a cross represented their religion."

"That theory has been discounted." He adjusted the temperature to make the cabin warmer. "Too savage to convey love. Probably the symbol of a trade union, just as that lady holding a torch was the icon of a light-and-power company."

He had produced dinner for them, and as they ate, she asked what they were really like, these strange people. Were they as primitive as her husband claimed?

"They were adolescent, self-deluding, and often barbaric."

If he meant military conflict, taking pride in the fact that their own civilization hadn't suffered such convulsions, she pointed out that it was rather difficult, after all, to conduct a land war in a spaceship.

Again he felt the need to impress her, for he was not all that sure she was his. She still concerned herself with her husband's welfare, though they had finally parted, far too amicably in his view. And she still grieved over her brother's death, which kept part of her inaccessible to him. These concerns were worrying, for she was not only beautiful and bright, she was also to be the means of his making his fortune. And so, hoping it would bring them closer and make her vote a certainty, he launched once again into his favorite theme: the awfulness of earthlings.

"These people invented gods of love, then murdered each other in religious wars. They drew boundaries to encompass nations, then swallowed each other like fish. They espoused freedom but kept half the globe in financial bondage, if not outright starvation. And we've come across an event so unbelievable it might be propaganda. It involves eight million people cooked in ovens."

"Why?" She looked up at him.

"The absolute certainty of fanatics. Even in their leisure they were fanatic. Their lust for sports was endless. A constant throwing, running, jumping, punching, and piling on top of each other. A mad adolescent compulsion to play."

"What about art? Aside from those cave drawings you always make fun of."

He admitted to the discovery of statues. A grumpy codger mouthing a cigar and holding up two fingers and a judge named Lincoln in a marble chair as if passing sentence on the planet. But was it really art to sculpt something so literal?

"There's this writer, Proust, who wrote a book too long to read, compared to the haiku, which, apparently, was too brief to grasp."

"But they found real sculpture in the jungle, didn't they?"

"Yes, statues of people copulating. A mirror would do as well. In Mexico they found intriguing twists of metal that may be art or just intriguing twists of metal."

"And music?"

"Maybe. Something called heavy metal sounds like the gnashing of gears."

Smiling again: "Is that what drove them to destroy themselves in a single day?"

He shook his head. "It wasn't quite like that."

"You have new information?"

"We do."

"About which you and my husband disagree."

"About which we are in total accord. Our computers calculate that the optimum population for a planet this size is two billion people. At the end they were twelve billion."

"I don't believe it."

"Pollution killed the food chain, and the temperature kept rising. There were droughts and floods, and the sea was emptied of fish. Land where food still grew was fought over like gold until that too was destroyed. Of course, once they killed themselves, things greatly improved, as you see."

The distant rim of sky was alive with slowly fading bloodstained light. An armada of black clouds like clusters of grief floated west to meet the night. She drank from a cup and put it down again. He knew that expression. The self-destruction of an entire race had brought her thoughts back to her brother. He'd perished when his spaceship had first reached this solar system. His module, with several others on board, had lost power and been pulled into the sun.

"You all right?" he asked, touching her shoulder. The wind howled in muffled grief. "Oh, dear, I see all this has upset you."

"Sorry."

To cheer her up he spoke again of their plans. For hundreds of generations their people had only known life aboard spaceships, huge city-states, fleets of them moving together through an apparently uninhabitable galaxy searching for what most of them had long since ceased to care about. Now that this place had been discovered, they would be curious enough to visit but too cautious to live there, for their ancestors had been forced to abandon their own planet when its sun had become unstable. Conventional wisdom said all planets were unsafe, for their history books, after all, described terrible floods, massive quakes, and destructive meteor showers. Who would wish to go back to all that? But coming as tourists to explore and enjoy this green and temperate place, they might soon be won over. Demand for property would then grow and profits soar. Therefore it would be unwise to dwell, in their brochures, on the self-destructive nature of earthlings. Better to appeal to some positive aspect. In fact, he had discovered something recently that he knew would please her.

"What do you mean?" she asked.

"In North America, in the basement of a medical building, they discovered a fifteen-year-old boy. He had been frozen for safe keeping until the cure for what he was dying of could be found."

"Oh, we did that ourselves once."

He nodded with sad amusement. "And the man was defrosted, cured, rehabilitated ..."

"And promptly killed one of his doctors."

"Cost us millions to resurrect one psychopath."

"Then we had to locate, arrest, try, convict, and put him to death again. What a mess."

"But this is different," he said. "I have tapes of the child's voice recording his life and thoughts just before he was put to sleep."

"How can that be?"

"A miracle. The cassettes were boxed in zinc, and so we can actually hear the voice of someone who lived six thousand earth years ago."

"Play them," she said excitedly. "Go on, play them for me."

He was already busy at the audio computer even as she spoke. He set the first tape in motion. They waited as the last dregs of light on the distant mountain range were absorbed into the night.

"... brill cleetonson lesserdon clat ebberport clee knotship squill ..."

He halted the machine with a soft curse. "Sorry. The translation switch wasn't turned on."

"So that's what English sounds like," she said.

"Yes, like a mouth full of marbles." He tapped a button. "Okay, here we go."

A voice of an earnest adolescent invaded their cabin as if he was seated beside them.

"... frenzy of welcome, his joy many times larger than ..."

He stopped the machine. "I'll just go back a bit." This was done, and then the boy's voice returned.

"... things I'd like to remember, such as Dipper. When we come home at night, he runs madly through the house in a frenzy of welcome, his joy so many times larger than his little body. And I want to remember Lorraine, across the street, so popular, so many men in cars drive up to take her out … On my fourteenth birthday there was a thunderstorm, and the deluge came down so hard it bounced to my knees. That night a shooting star whipped by in terrible silence. I often think about civilizations out there on other planets and whether, when we finally meet, they'll be like we are. Perhaps when I come back—if I come back—we'll have made contact and found out just how superior they are to us. When I wake up in the future, I will have left so much behind. But I bet I know what will always be with us: *Crime and Punishment* and, of course, *War and Peace*."

He stopped the tape. "Note the disillusionment in one so young. He knows there will always be crime and war."

"Please, I want to hear the rest."

He set it going again.

"I would like to remember my father, but he died in a car crash when I was three. My mother will be by my side until I go into that cold sleep to come awake a hundred, perhaps a thousand years from now. All who are here today will be gone. How lonely that will be. I'll have to make new friends. And my mother's love. When I get lonely, I'll remember how wonderful it was, and that will keep her memory alive to warm me always … And my friends Aleck and Carl will be gone too. How odd to think that I will have slept their lives away. Will I find their graves, I wonder? And my mother's? To stand there and tell her that I've come back safely. And in the future, will there be girls like Lorraine? So friendly, so pretty. I found her one spring morning sitting in the sun on West Hill. Fidgety butterflies floated about while a gentle wind petted the grass. We talked. She pretended to need my help when getting to her feet. Her skin cocoa colored by the summer sun. Next week she'll be eighteen."

Halting the tape: "Just let me jump ahead a bit."

Soon the boy spoke again. "… knocking on a closed door to an even …"

He ran it back slightly.

"But these days I'm frightened of the night. Much pain. Little sleep. I put the lamp on because sometimes all I can hear is my heartbeat like the discreet knocking on a closed door, a door to an even greater darkness until it opens and I am let in. Can anyone ever return through that door? Well, if I do, I'll be famous, I guess. Someday, when I finally die a second time, won't it be odd to have on my gravestone TIMOTHY ANDERSON 1971–1986 and then something like 2100–2170. But if I die and live again, will I be any wiser? And will the girls in the future care for me? Will they be like Lorraine, so calm and mature that I will feel a child in their eyes? Of course, I might seem like a freak, not understanding their language and unable to be understood. It all makes sense to me now. 'The undiscovered country from whose bourn no traveler returns, puzzles the will and make us rather bear those ills we have than fly to others we know not of.'"

"There, isn't that poetry?" she insisted. "He's quoting poetry."

He shrugged as the boy continued.

"They threw a going-away party for me on the Fourth of July. Even Lorraine was there. She pushed my wheelchair onto the back porch where we all watched the fireworks. When she left, she kissed my cheek. I marvel that all the men aren't in love with her. Or maybe they are. As I am. When everyone went home, I looked at the mess and said the best time to have a party was on the day the world ends, for then no one would have to clean up. Mother cried. Too much wine, she said. And I cried too, for I knew I was going off to leave her all by herself. So we just sat there side by side under the moon while the wind spoke of what a wonderful thing it was to be alive … I don't think I'll be able to record much more. Pain again. Very bad. No sleep. From my window I could watch for as long as I wished one of the many spenders of this life, the night sky engulfed with silvers of fire."

The machine clicked off, and they sat without speaking. A savage wind buffeted the mountain. She was crying. He always felt helpless at moments like this.

"Are you okay?"

He was about to touch her when she turned to him. "We must start now," she cried.

"To do what?"

"To do what? To bring him back again, of course. Why haven't you done this already? This is monumental."

"Listen, please."

"I want this boy alive, now."

"We can't. He's dead."

"Of course he's dead. But all we have to do—"

"You don't think he stayed frozen for six thousand years, do you? Refrigeration stopped soon after human life did."

She closed her eyes, her hand to her mouth. He cursed himself for even mentioning the boy. His ego had been too big to leave room for common sense.

Finally, she cried out, "Oh, that awful howling." As if the mountain heard her, the onslaught paused. She grew frightened. "What's that on the window?"

"Just snow, my dear. Just beautiful, falling snow." He took her hand. "Come. I'll take you someplace where it's morning."

They chased and caught the sunset, then pressed on until it became early evening, which turned finally into a bright, wide, fulsome day as the glistening Atlantic passed beneath them. Then a seemingly endless forest spread itself across a continent, and at last the Rockies came at them out of the morning glare like a tidal wave. They landed on a beach and stepped down carefully into warm sand near blue water. The only sound was the tumbling waves, and with each a shelf of foam slid out of the sea, spread wide and white, and was sucked back again. The sun that had killed her brother now hugged them lovingly.

"Let's sit here, shall we?"

Her face was lifeless. "All right."

"I'm sorry about that misunderstanding."

She repeatedly lifted and let fall white sand from her palm. "My darling, we're not being honest with ourselves. There is so much here to uncover and learn from."

A cold fear gripped him. "Hang on. If we let them renew their contract, we'll lose this place to those artifact fanatics. We'll never get it back. And what of our people, waiting their whole lives away never to be warmed by the sun and, as you said, made love to by the wind? This paradise will make all of us happy and some of us rich. Why throw it away because of the sad musings of a sick child?"

She glared at him. Or was she just squinting in the sun.

"What changed your mind?" he asked.

"His lovely voice, for a start."

"I'm sorry he had a lovely voice. But I repeat: let's not lose all this because of him." With a touch of menace: "I do hope you're with me on this one."

"Am I with you?"

"That's what I asked."

Again she played with the sand. "Of course I am. I want my share as much as you do."

"So we are in agreement?"

"Yes, my love, we are."

"Good. Now let's forget all this, take our clothes off, and go for a dip. It'll be the first time for us ever."

And at last she smiled. "But only up to our knees, mind you. Who knows what lurks under the surface. Oh dear, I left my skin cream in the ship."

Resigned: "Okay, I'll go."

"No, no, let me. And when I get back, I want you naked and ready." Then mocking his tone of menace, she said, "I hope you're with me on this one."

"Indeed, I am. What with the sun's heat, and yours, I might melt away if I'm not careful."

She rose and trudged through the sand, climbed the steps, closed the door with a reassuring thump. Seated on the couch, she pressed a button on her wristwatch. "Come on, surely you're not so busy taking your clothes off that you can't hear ..."

At last his voice, gruff and businesslike, filled the module. "Yes, what is it?"

"It's only me, love. Sorry, but I've changed my vote. I've joined the artifact fanatics."

"You can't. This is stupid."

"Perhaps, but I'm flying back right now. I'll send someone to pick you up."

"Don't you dare!" he shouted.

"Sorry."

She saw him running toward her. "Darling, don't. The door's locked."

He pounded with his fist. "I'll kill you."

"Yes, I thought you might. Oh, and another thing, I plan to tell my husband that I would very much like to resume our marriage."

"You're joking."

"No, I'm not. Now stand back, please."

"All this because of a little wimp who died eons ago."

"I'm afraid so."

"All because of his damned voice?"

"If I hadn't known, I would have sworn it was my brother."

"Oh, no."

"Sorry. And while you're waiting, why not enjoy the splendor of this place. You were right about one thing. After our almost endless search, we've found it at last. Paradise."

Make My Bed and Light the Light

Though Josh could recall telling himself not to forget, he couldn't be sure he'd listened carefully enough to remember. On Columbus Avenue, after hooking his cane on a trash basket, he plunged his hands into his pockets. Out came an old movie stub and a paper clip. These he flung into the trash. Ah, and here was that elusive receipt from his demon dentist. He filed it into his important-papers pocket inside his jacket near his heart. But the all-important dry-cleaning stub (orange with a perforated edge) was gone. Blast. He would have to go all the way back. Blast.

He went several steps before returning to retrieve his cane. Setting off again, he was startled by the unflattering sight of his transparent self in a pane of glass wearing his rakish (or was it buffoonish?) commodore's cap with that embarrassing expression of grumpy resolve—far from the noble profile of Caesar and more like that bloated fishmonger's face of Socrates. Store windows were an intrusion into one's private life, and in the next reflection, a few stores down, he was dismayed by his unrhythmic stride as if on a jaunty trudge through snow.

Like a stargazer, he stood in the lobby watching numbers light up: 3 then 2 then L. Inside, with both hands on his cane, he waited to be lifted. He was lowered. When a lady entered from the basement, he removed his cap. When she got off at 17, he pulled it on again. At the top floor, standing in front of 29F, he fumbled with his key long enough for an impatient someone inside to pull the door open for him. His son, Harvey, returned to the couch and reclaimed his scotch and soda. He was in bare feet, torn jeans, and one of his new, almost-fluorescent blue shirts. His grandson, Billy, in soiled shorts and T-shirt, was sitting on the floor with his back to the couch.

"What did you forget this time, Pop?" Harvey asked without looking at him.

"Nothing."

"Short walk, then."

"Short walk." Josh stood engrossed, then asked, "What's love?"

"Oh, not again."

"Well, what is it?"

"Nothing."

"Love is nothing?"

"You got it in one, Pop." Then Harvey shouted, "Wow!" put down his drink, and clapped.

"What's triple break point?"

Billy answered, "It can't be explained, Gramps. You've just got to know."

Vivian appeared from the kitchen area. "Josh, dear, you're blocking my view."

"Pop, sit down," Harvey snapped.

He did, on the couch, next to his son, to watch as a drumbeat of ground strokes stretched the tension until it was snapped by the crowd's thunder.

"What does it mean, broken at love?"

No one heard him, for in a rare moment of unity his family unleashed a violent cheer. It was sad to see them stricken into brief postures of total joy knowing that nothing but a sports event could evoke such passion. Instead of Harvey introducing the boy to Chopin or Dickens, it was Billy who hooked his father and stepmother on banal TV programs and loud pop songs whose lyrics Josh could not for the life of him decipher. Billy had even hooked his father, a baseball addict, on this odd game of half-ballet, half–paddle ball.

Josh kept to a world they knew nothing of: books. Yet all things new tugged at him, and so he was curious about this high-tossing sport of genteel savagery.

"Ask him later about break points, Josh," Vivian said and went back to the kitchen.

Though she was to some extent … what was the word? Honorary? No. Ornamental? Didn't sound right. Trophy. That was it. Though she was to some extent a trophy wife, there was much more to her than that. Yes, a bit of a princess sometimes, yet she was genuinely friendly to everyone and devoted to her stepson. Harvey's first wife, Selma, who worked in a dentist's office, had put up with Harvey for twelve years and then, announcing the marriage was over, had walked out with Billy, who later had moved back with his father because he disliked his mother's new husband. Viv had been a professional model (color photos of her in grotesque clothes hung in the hallway), but she'd retired after her engagement to Harvey. At thirty-six she was still too thin for Josh's taste, and her beauty seemed somewhat fragile for this knockabout world and, as he imagined it, the rough justice of their marriage bed. Josh liked her all the more for her fussing over him, perhaps because her own father had left home when she was five and returned only in her dreams.

You could even say Harvey owned a trophy apartment: too many rooms for too few people. And though he and his family barely noticed the view that Josh loved, not having had one worth a damn in any place he had ever lived. Standing on their balcony, he could see, far to the right, the George Washington Bridge, looking as if constructed from an expensive Erector Set. Far to the left, barely visible, easily overlooked and all alone on her tiny island, was a thumb-size Statue of Liberty. Across the ash-gray Hudson, beyond a down-market New Jersey, were the low, distant, misty hills of Pennsylvania.

The question of break points was forgotten when the TV camera intruded upon a white-haired lady in the visitor's box who had played in this very tournament six decades ago. The commentator said she was eighty-four years young. Josh smiled, for he was soon to be ninety.

This drew the old man into a long-ago life when he'd hauled blocks of ice on his shoulder from the back of a truck up dim stairways to gallop weightlessly down again, with his tongs and canvas cloth, to reemerge among pushcarts and punishing heat, to lift yet another steaming chunk of winter up to another dingy kitchen while, a few miles away in Forest Hills, multitudes had been cheering the white-haired lady's teenage deeds.

He too had wanted to make a great noise in this world. Like most people, he'd remained barely audible. He would have loved to teach American history, to plumb its depths and call attention to the blunders and plunders of each administration—in particular, to describe how the Great Depression had come about, dropping the bottom out of so many lives and killing his own chance to attend college. How hundreds had stood mute outside the stock exchange waiting for a miracle that had never come. In the middle of a drained lake in Central Park, shantytowns had grown. People without shoes had tied cardboard to their feet, and Josh had eaten only potatoes for a month while many had eaten less or nothing. Such fear. Such disbelief. Josh had outrun a man with a knife who had demanded his wallet. On another occasion he'd come to the aid of an old woman struggling to stop two thugs from stealing her purse. He, against all odds, had been given a miraculous job mopping floors in Macy's on Herald Square. Then he'd gotten a promotion to shipping and, years later, to toys, where he'd sold Erector Sets and electric trains.

Recently he and Billy had had a chat. "The Great Depression, was that a real downer, Gramps?"

"Boy, was it ever. Runaway greed made everyone poor." Here, at last, had been a chance to tell his grandson of stupidity in high places and how banks could trap and hold your money as if it were their own. But the boy had lost interest.

"Was it cool playing with the toys, Gramps?"

"Toys? Didn't have any."

"In Macy's, I mean."

"Ah. Kids loved watching the trains go through those little tunnels and stop at tiny stations. Great fun."

"You work there long?"

"And how."

"How long?"

"Sixty-one years."

"Sixty-one years?"

"You said it. Try standing on your feet for sixty-one years. I told stories to the kids. This train is bringing fathers home to Peekskill; that train is taking Mrs. Swartz to see her son, Herbert. They loved it. Parents too. Even my boss. Of course he *lived* in Peekskill. In 1985 forced retirement ended, so I stayed on. What else was there? My friends? Dead and buried. Everyone's mortal. But some are more mortal than others. Some die young. Some younger even. Tragic. I still talk to my friends. But now they don't answer. So I talk to your family. They don't answer either. So you're my audience, kid. Sorry about that. When Harvey was your age, I advised him to teach history. Americans know beans about history, not even their own. Instead he goes into the market and makes a bundle."

The boy had smiled. "Good thing too. Took you in. Pays my school fees. Gives to charity."

"Gives to Viv. *She* gives to charity. Like all those dresses she wears just once."

The lad had seemed amused by his glamorous stepmother with her charge accounts at five restaurants, three department stores, and two taxi firms and who had more clothes than closets.

"Hey, Dad did good."

"Okay. To him, I take off my hat. Provides for the family. Enough for ten families. Yet you wear the same T-shirt all year round. Go figure."

Mistaking this for praise, Billy had thrown two quick jabs just short of the old man's belt buckle. "Gramps, you're the best. You totally are. Did you fight in the war?"

"Wanted to but was 4-F. Heart murmur."

"What's that?"

"They thought it was a leaky valve. Turned out it was just humming to itself."

"A real downer. You would've beat the living crap out of those Germans."

A few more quick jabs and he had been gone, though Josh had had more to say. A good kid but with no real interests in life. Thought it was cool not to study. Harvey was different. He worked hard, harder when profits loomed. Yet he too had a closed mind. An early closing. In a three-piece suit, Harvey could impersonate a serious person. After hours, he was an undergraduate again. Lived the good life without giving a thought to those who never would. Very American that. How had they become so different, he and his son? Had he failed as a father? Or was it due to Sara's death when Harvey was still young?

The day he'd made a mammoth killing in the market, Harvey had come to Macy's one afternoon and taken Josh to lunch. They'd gone to Keane's Chop House where recorked wine bottles hung from the ceiling waiting to be claimed by customers when they returned for another meal. A Bordeaux to die for had been taken down and placed on their table.

"Dad, I got news for you: we're rich."

"Good. Hope it lasts till the check comes."

"Josh, you took care of me all those years; now I want to take care of you."

"That's sweet, but I have a job."

"Which I want you to quit. Come on. Just seeing you standing behind that damned toy counter makes my knees hurt. Quit and move in with us. I mean it. Look, your entire salary wouldn't pay my income tax. And, Pop, what will it look like if I retire before you do? That's a joke."

"Not necessarily."

"Will you quit and move in? We have plenty of room."

"I'll think about it."

"Pop, you think too much."

"I'll think about that too."

No thank you was what he'd said, and he'd kept saying it for years. Then Harvey had remarried, and his new wife, Vivian, had insisted, phoned again and again to say how welcomed he would be, how much she wanted him to live with them, how much she needed him to live with them. At last the old man had relented. The solitude he'd always loved was wearing thin. His old neighborhood had become a new one. Familiar faces were disappearing. Friends in his building had died. Shops he'd loved had closed. Others he had no use for had opened. It had been time for a change. By stealth, it had already come. So he'd moved out of his apartment on Thirtieth Street, sending on, with his clothes and other things, 943 paperbacks (mostly histories and novels) and 408 classical CDs (from Thomas Tallis to Arvo Pärt). He'd handed in his resignation and suffered a good-bye party he didn't want held in toys by a staff he barely knew who had given him gifts he didn't need, which he'd taken away in a Macy's shopping bag. When he'd arrived at Harvey's apartment on West Seventieth Street only Billy, to his surprise, had been there to greet him.

Josh had come to regret this move. His family was probably as dysfunctional as most in America. He hoped not for his country's sake. Yet this was hardly a consolation. Life for them was an ongoing search for hyperactive entertainment, and their presence in his life was not unlike a ceaseless but inaudible public address announcement. Madame de Sevigne wrote about this in one of her letters, how some people deprived her of solitude without affording her company.

"Listen, Harvey," Josh had tried to explain once, while eating Chinese takeout with the family, "it's when the good times roll that we need to put the brakes on."

"Stop prosperity?" His son's mock outrage had caused general merriment. "Try telling that to stockholders." He'd taken a second helping of sweet-and-sour prawns.

"Marx said that boom and bust would always…"

"Dad, you're a child of the Great Crash. Today we have systems in place so that …"

Billy had broken open his fortune cookie. "Hey, guys. Chinese proverb. Those who despise money will end up sponging on their friends."

"Yes." Harvey had pumped his fist in the air. "Hear that, Josh? Well done, Billy. More wine, Viv?"

The TV had been switched on as they ate so they could half listen to and glance occasionally at the fraught faces in a slowly plodding soap opera. This intrusion had held the room hostage for brief stretches of time, giving way again to family revels of cross-purpose conversations, triumphant laughter, and, because Viv insisted they use them, complaints about chopsticks. Josh had finished, excused himself, and gone to bed to read in peace.

When you get older, they say, you need less sleep. Long ago he'd needed eight hours in bed to get eight hours of sleep. Now he needed nine to achieve six—if he was lucky. That they don't tell you. As a result, for the last three decades, he had become a reluctant witness to the small hours. In his new home, modern and polished with elevators and doormen, the night sounds were worse: the buzzing expressway, the chug of a train, a mournful horn from the river, and the howl of that ceaseless grieving wind. Time stopped even as the clock ticked. At night, though he would never admit this to anyone, he was more lonely than ever.

He tried to reignite his long-lost fear of death. Was there anything better to increase a thirst for life than to be reminded that all must end? That inclination in old age to glide through the days, detached from care, numb to pleasure, was not for him. In the invasion of Normandy gliders had been used by Allied troops to capture Pegasus Bridge. He'd tossed gliders as a child, but they'd always darted off course and sped into the ground. Better were those paper planes with rubber bands that spun aloft to flutter about and execute a graceful bouncing crash. Why were his thoughts wandering like this? So often too. Was it attention deficit, of all things? Another worry.

Each week, then, was a rerun of the one before. Harvey drank too much and was forever checking his cell phone. Viv went off shopping as if new clothes kept her young. Billy drank Coke and stared at the noisy TV screen. The family argued, took sides, changed sides, fought again, made up, or sulked. Then they all came together at whatever athletic event Billy wanted to watch.

"Great shot." Harvey put down his scotch and soda to applaud as the crowd thundered, and Viv came in for the replay to see what she had missed.

"What's deuce?" Josh asked. No one answered.

When the match ended, Harvey, never one to lose time, asked, "What's for dinner?"

"I thought we'd have Indian."

"So what were you doing in the kitchen all this time?"

"Looking for the takeout menu."

"I want chicken korma," Billy told his father, who did the phoning.

"That's the one thing in this world I can always count on. Viv, what's yours?"

Their habit of having food brought in annoyed Josh. This evening, as Harvey was about to dial the restaurant, a memory bubbled up—two days ago, was it?—of Shelley's voice on the phone with a message.

"By the way, Sheldon called," he said, feeling overheated and unworthy.

Harvey flung out an abrupt "What?"

"When?" his wife asked.

"Shell?" Billy looked up. "He called?"

Vivian's uncle, Sheldon Zimmerman, always came to town without prior warning. He was wealthy and well liked, by this family at least. Having none of his own, he adored children. Often he would treat Billy to a movie or a ball game, and he knew Hollywood gossip; he had a brother who worked for MGM.

Harvey stood up. "Where's he staying, Pop?"

"He has a new cell phone. I wrote down the number."

"Where?"

"In my room."

"Get it."

"I'm going." Among the papers on his desk he unearthed the orange dry-cleaning stub that he had come back for but then forgotten about. He tucked it away for safekeeping and looked everywhere and under everything three times. With a sigh, he trundled back to confess that the slip of paper was missing.

Harvey's voice jumped octaves, swelled by decibels. Sheldon would not call again. He was like that; he would drive back to Trenton and be heard from no more. Vivian phoned the two hotels he had used in the past. No luck. A furious Harvey disrupted his father's room like a police raid, in vain.

"What a stupid thing," he whined. "In the future make notes. Stick one on the fridge and one on your nose. Oh, hell." And he hit the wall a mighty blow with the TV Guide.

Dinner was grim, and Josh escaped to his room as soon as he could. Sure enough, Sheldon didn't call again. With the worst timing possible, the next day was Josh's birthday, and Harvey had booked tickets to the theater. That morning, stating the obvious, Vivian remarked how sad it was that her uncle wouldn't be joining them.

Last year they had celebrated with a boat ride to Bear Mountain, but it had rained and rained. This year they had chosen *The Phantom of the Opera*. Then they would go to a restaurant and give Granddad his presents. The plan was to meet at the theater, and Josh, so as not to be a burden, insisted he would get there on his own, especially now that they were barely talking to him.

He overslept, having spent much of the night reading a book on twentieth-century America, gripped all the more by having lived through those historic events. Born in 1910, he could just remember that reckless era of runaway wealth. His ninety years were crammed with stunning wonders and horrors beyond consolation. Yet he could never manage to share much of this with his family. To them the past was comprised of movie favorites, legends created by American athletes, out-of-date motor cars, and household bric-a-brac like their old samovar now made into a lamp or a black antique telephone resting in its high carriage and hooked up to receive calls in their kitchen, though far too cumbersome for dialing numbers. So he alone in the family was left to worry about and witness anew those forgotten lessons of history as they were disastrously repeated.

He had learned to read and write at a knife-scarred desk with an inkwell filled from the spout of a metal can poured by a fellow student. Often the mixture had thickened so when Josh had dipped his pen and prepared to write, he'd pulled across the desk and onto his copybook a black thread of glutinous ink. Today Billy used a computer. But had he learned to type? Two fingers only, while three were needed to hold a pen. Now there was progress for you.

When Josh was a boy, a clamoring biplane had landed in an open field beside his cousin's house on Long Island. A man in goggles had climbed out, bought gas from a farmer, and asked, "Hey, kid, which way to New York?" Pointing in what he'd hoped was the right direction, he'd watched the pilot wave as he'd risen heroically into an empty sky. Decades later, when Josh had described this magical event, his son had barely listened. Only when men had bounced about on the moon had Harvey briefly come alert to the world around him. Nor did Josh's family respond to his descriptions of Manhattan before air conditioning had rescued it. How, in Central Park at night, as far as the eye could see, families had slept on blankets to escape the heat. How he'd often laid his bedding on his fire escape, amid silence and sirens, to catch a stir of air. He'd even dragged his mattress to the roof, once the sunbaked tar had dried, to spend a starless night until a cool breeze had nudged him awake to squint at the silver glare of sunrise on the East River. And Viv grumbled because the hum of the bedroom air conditioner was not soft enough.

When Josh emerged from his room on the morning of his birthday, he was amazed to see Harvey, who should have left for work by now, standing in his business suit, a cup of coffee in hand, gazing through the window and, dressed for the office as he was, seeming oddly out of place in his own home. He glanced at his father and then at the Hudson again. A motionless seagull slid by, white, regal, brazen.

"Some view, eh," Josh said, hoping to get a response from his philistine son.

"Haven't done too badly, have we, Josh? This place, those trips to Disneyland, Billy's college fees safe in the bank, our BMW in the garage, not bad at all, I'd say." He took a careful sip while holding the saucer at belt level. "We're floating on high like that bird out there." Another sip. "Am I right, Pop? You've seen it all. These are great times, no? Republicans in power. The economy booming. A new millennium. Two thousand and counting. Bet you've never seen better. What do you think?" He looked at Josh and waited.

The old man didn't have the heart to say what he thought. Instead, a distant feeling came back, surprising him: tenderness for his son and a need to shelter him.

"Not too bad. Got my health. Viv's got her looks. You got your job, and the kid's okay. Needs a new T-shirt is all. So what can I tell ya? Mazel tov."

At the phrase "got your job," there was a brief disconnect in his son's eyes as when, due to a cable glitch, someone freezes on TV and just as quickly moves again. He smiled.

"I bow to your greater wisdom."

"Just don't spill your coffee."

"You're in a good mood."

He put the cup and saucer on the table and, with uncomfortable solemnity, wished his father a happy birthday. Pausing at the door, attaché case in hand and with his gray hair needing a trim, he said, "At the theater, then?"

"I'll be there."

"Got your ticket?"

Josh patted the vest pocket.

"Haven't left yet?" Vivian had entered the room. "Is something wrong?"

She wore a blue silk kimono and slippers with heels.

"Wanted to wish him a happy ninetieth, okay?"

"We do that tonight."

"No harm done. Well, off to work then with sword and shield."

"You sure nothing's wrong? You're not sleeping well."

"Got things on my mind. That's how you stay ahead. Don't need much sleep anyway."

She looked at Josh as if to say, *What's to be done with this man?*

Harvey held up his hand. "Viv, stop worrying. Have breakfast. Go shopping. It pains me to see you frown. Pop, take over. I have to leave."

"Maybe kiss her first," said Josh, "then go."

His son stood gripping his attaché case. Then moved to give her a quick peck on the brow, a firm pat on her shoulder; then with a wave like a politician he was gone.

"Drives me nuts when he gets this way. Doesn't talk, doesn't smile. It's some problem at work. I just know it is. Will he be all right? You nod. Always so calm. Don't you ever worry about anything? Yes, you worry about the country."

"Correct."

"Why?"

"No memory, impossible for a nation to learn without memory."

"So he'll be all right?"

"Sure."

She scrambled a hand through her hair and laughed at the state she was in. "Oh, and happy birthday, Josh. You're amazing at ninety."

"*You're* amazing at thirty-six," he said, ogling his eyebrows and flicking an invisible cigar.

As always, she laughed when praised. Due to their poor treatment of him of late, she let it slip out: "I love you, Josh. I really do."

"Vell," he said, "not ha moment too soon."

That afternoon Josh was mulling over the events of the morning when Harvey's words "Got your ticket?" popped up. Yes, he must hurry and pick up his suit. Later, in front of the dry cleaners, he couldn't recall if he had remembered to bring it, and so again, there in the street, his cane hanging from the trash basket, he plunged his hands into his pockets, searching. Blast.

To hell with it. He would go straight to the theater in his old sport jacket. Who cared anyway? So what would he do now with all this free time on his hands? Buy a magazine. Why not? Opening his wallet, he found among the tens and fives and credit card receipts and torn movie tickets and cash register slips, the ever-elusive orange dry-cleaning stub. He made an about-turn in front of the newspaper store and performed his rickety jaunt down the block. He and the old Jewish tailor discussed the woes of the world and how he had lost the stub and found it again. "You don't need it," barked the owner. "Why do you need it? You, I know. Show me your face; I give you your suit. Simple."

Why hadn't he thought of that? Blast. Well, a lesson learned. Josh handed him the stub.

"Wait," he cried, "give it back."

"No, I need it."

"The hell you do." Josh snatched it away and made for the street, the owner calling after him, "You crazy person."

At the corner, he pushed coins into a pay phone, removed his glasses to use the left lens to magnify the keyboard, and dialed the number he had written on the back of the stub. When he put his bifocals back on, his hearing aids beeped in protest.

"Shelley?" he shouted. "Josh. Found it. Your number. Where are you? What street? Okay, don't go nowhere. It's a surprise. Put on your suit. I'll pick you up seven sharp in a taxi. What? Listen, if I told you, it wouldn't be a surprise. I'm coming. Be ready."

Back in the tailor shop, Josh borrowed a pen, wrote the street number of the hotel on the back of his left hand, paid the dry-cleaning bill, and marched home with his suit over his arm like a cellophane body bag. When he reappeared, dressed in his best, he tipped his cap in the lobby to Mrs. Kelley, put it on, and then took it off again to wave as if from a desert island to a distant ship. The taxi stopped. He opened the door, threw his cane in, put his cap on, and backed his way onto the seat.

Shelley was seventy-five, bald, wore a polka dot bow tie and rode across town as if sitting for his portrait. He was good with children, with adults less so.

"Josh, you're still alive. I'm glad for you."

"Don't tempt fate, or you might have to pay for the cab."

"Where you taking me?"

"To the theater."

"Why?"

"It's my birthday."

"Your birthday? Mazel tov. How old?"

"Ninety."

"*Ninety*? Really? Well, you look terrific."

"You went last to an optometrist when?"

"Level with me, what's the secret of long life?"

"At my age, who can remember?"

"Well, you do look terrific."

"Convince the family. I know how I look."

"They'll be there?"

"Of course. What are you, my date?"

There was a crowd out front trying to get in. Handing Shelley his ticket, Josh sent him to his seat. "Knock 'em dead, kid. I'll be there in a minute."

Shelley was delighted. A surprise party with him the surprise.

"I'll fake ignorance. 'Harvey,' I'll say, 'as I live and breathe.'"

"Good, now go already."

He hurried off, holding his ticket aloft like a raffle winner. Josh went to the window marked This Performance. "I'm waiting for a return."

"Sorry, none yet," said a man in a bow tie like Shelley's. Josh stepped aside and waited, both hands pressing on his cane. A voice boomed that the curtain was going up in five minutes. Then three. Then one. Latecomers hurried. The lobby expanded as it emptied. Josh returned to the window. The man in the bow tie said he was sorry. A muffled show tune. The fun had started. He turned and did his hobbled walk into the street.

The name of the restaurant had slipped his mind again. Blast. Keane's Chop House? Maybe. Lindy's on Broadway? *Don't be stupid.* It had closed years ago, though he could still taste their strawberry cheesecake. An old waiter there with a case of the shakes would jiggle a cup of coffee to their table, poor the spillage from the saucer back into the cup, place it down, and say, "Enjoy." The coffee at Horn and Hardart had come from a spout like a dolphin's head. Also closed years ago. It was there he'd told Sara, his future wife, how he and his parents had hid for days in an attic in Odessa while hearing horses and gunshots in the street. She'd listened, fingers to her lips, then beamed as they'd escaped from the pogrom onto a crowded Greek cargo ship.

Sara had been in jewelry on the ground floor. The first time he'd come down from toys and had seen her behind the counter, her beauty had struck him with harmless lightning. She'd lived in Newark and had a gift for gaiety. *In Newark she would need it,* he'd told himself. Equally important, she had been able to subdue all worries with the touch of her hand and a cuddling smile. And innocent. So innocent she'd listed herself in the phone book not, as most women had, with only the initial of her first name but first, last, and middle name in full.

Fate had done all it could to dim her optimism. Her father had been a suicide in the depression, and her firstborn had died in childbirth. Yet nothing had been able to diminish what was special about her. Only death had done that, taking her (it was like a sick joke) in the terminal building of Idlewild Airport. A heart attack at forty-seven. It had taken a long time for the sun to rise again. Even when Josh had somewhat recovered, he'd felt like that mythical muscleman and dimwit Atlas, who was forever crushed beneath an uncaring world. His own burden had seemed heavier still, filled as it had been with longing. To this day he had never been able to lessen the sadistic perfection of her absence.

Tears blurred the buffoon in the store window. "Stop crying, would you. You're a grown man and then some. Fully grown despite an inch of shrinkage. So stop. Okay. Promise? I promise. Okay."

Having cheered up a notch or two, he remembered what he had forgotten and directed his antic lope back to the theater to ask the time of the intermission. That done, he moved on, probing his useless memory for the restaurant's name. His plan was to return at the end of the first act to reassure them he wasn't lying facedown in the gutter somewhere and to ask them, ever so casually, to remind him where they all planned to eat. Harvey, of course, would berate him yet again for refusing to buy a cell phone. But he didn't want them always calling to make sure he wasn't dead.

"I don't have dementia. I can still walk, am housebroken, more or less. So what do I need a phone for?" He would never admit, even when Viv tried to lend him hers, that he never could get the damned thing to work.

Anyway, it would be fun strolling about until the intermission, so he headed west into the dim and shoddy midtown streets. He loved best the New York of his youth. Manageable by day or night. Though the city had changed for the worse, it gripped him still with a rare vista down an empty avenue, entangled multitudes with their dizzying busyness, faces seen once and never again. In the old days kids had played stickball in the street or swum in the Hudson. There had been Ping Pong clubs on Broadway and free lunch at the sandwich table if you bought a beer at the bar. Always, of course, there had been endless waste and want, loud calamities, noise, and dirt. But always there had also been those lights towering into the night sky.

A friend, Gabby, who had long since passed on, had once lived along here somewhere. He'd worked backstage as a sound technician and one evening had led Josh through a side door so he could watch Frank Fay, a beguiling comedian who, with effortless hilarity, played a lovable eccentric in a play called *Harvey*.

Where was that door leading into the theater? Here perhaps. He stepped into a lit passageway of trash cans and billboard signs. A voice behind him called out, "Hey, wait up." Was it Billy? What had gone wrong to bring his grandson here? Josh turned and saw someone in a black hood like a medieval monk perhaps, except he was holding a Coke bottle by the neck. He said, "You a stage-door Johnny, I bet, waitin' fo' one of dem show girls. Well, my friend, you in luck, 'cause I know where their dressin' room's at fo' you to get an au-*toe*-graph. Lovely ladies, yes, sir. The door's on down dis way."

"Stand back." Josh held his cane like a drawn sword.

"Look at you now. A shining knight without no armor."

The man pulled on the cane as if he suddenly wanted it for himself, and Josh stumbled forward as the Coke bottle was swung aloft. The night sky cracked open, and molten lava consumed him in a scorching flame.

A police officer was bending down. "Can you hear me, sir?" People stood watching like ticket holders. An ambulance was there as though hailed like a cab. Inside, a nice man took his pulse. Josh, lying on his back, was rolled down a long corridor in a bright building. The ceiling kept passing above him; then a large lightbulb came and went, then the ceiling again passing above him, another lightbulb, then the ceiling again. His good suit was wet with blood, his wallet gone, his cap and cane as well. Blast. How would he get to his birthday dinner? A nurse offered a lopsided smile. It was his wife come back to say, *Don't worry, Josh; it will all be put right.*

Except for death, he thought. How dumb was that? Of course, except for death. Death could never be put right.

Handled and hurt, bothered and bandaged, he was finally left alone with his pain in a high bed in a big room where others were bundled like him in blankets.

"Were you mugged, Pops?" asked a black youth in a neck brace.

"Where am I?" Josh asked.

"Welcome to Bellevue." Then, for some reason, Josh remembered. Cent'Annai, the restaurant on Carmine Street. Of course. He called out, and that same nurse came back, the one with his wife's smile.

"Cent'Annai."

"You Italian?" she asked. "Me, I'm Italian. So you're a hundred years old, are you?"

There was a disturbance somewhere, and she hurried off. The youth spoke again. "Hey, Pops, you're a survivor."

"As luck would have it."

"Day is all survivors here. One big beat-up family. Need somethin', sing out, you hear, and I'll help, okay?"

Josh wanted to tell his new friend that this was his birthday and he had to be in the Village to celebrate. But he was alone again with his throbbing head as well as the warm mystery of this strange place. Then she was there, her worrying face close to him, asking how he felt. Was he in pain? Sara smiled, and the pain was gone.

"Joshua, remember our trip together. We were so happy."

"You mean ..."

"We flew to that beach—where was it?—and the water was so warm, and we could see our toes at the bottom so clearly."

"No. You died at the airport."

"Did I? Oh dear, I'm sorry."

"I tried to bring you back, get you breathing again."

It cherished him once more, that smile. "Oh, yes, I recall now. I remember you kissing me. So lovely ... so special."

He had so much more to tell her, but there was a brief scream from a far corner, and he slipped away, fatigue lifting him down like a waterfall, and for the first time in decades he slept without waking.